# Catch all the

*MacMouse Brings Down the House*
Linda Phillips Teitel

*The Pup Who Cried Wolf*
Chris Kurtz

# Angus
# Bring
### the

*Ang*

# ANIMAL TALES

# Angus MacMouse Brings Down the House

**Linda Phillips Teitel**

illustrations by Guy Francis

**BLOOMSBURY**

NEW YORK BERLIN LONDON

First published in the United States of America in May 2010
by Bloomsbury Books for Young Readers
www.bloomsburykids.com

For information about permission to reproduce selections from this book, write to
Permissions, Bloomsbury BFYR, 175 Fifth Avenue, New York, New York 10010

Library of Congress Cataloging-in-Publication Data
Teitel, Linda Phillips.
Angus MacMouse brings down the house / by Linda Phillips Teitel. — 1st U.S. ed.
p.      cm.
Summary: Angus MacMouse's dreams of escaping his dreary life of hunger and cold on
the streets of New York come true when he happens into the Brooklyn Opera House,
creates a sensation, and makes a new friend, Rosemary.
ISBN 978-1-59990-490-0 (paperback) • ISBN 978-1-59990-493-1 (hardcover)
[1. Mice—Fiction.   2. Human–animal relationships—Fiction.   3. Opera—
Fiction.   4. Singers—Fiction.   5. Adventure and adventurers—Fiction.   6. Brooklyn
(New York, N.Y.)—Fiction.]   I. Title.
PZ7.T23218Ang 2010      [Fic]—dc22      2009036039

Book design by Danielle Delaney
Typeset by Westchester Book Composition
Printed in the U.S.A. by Worldcolor Fairfield, Pennsylvania
2  4  6  8  10  9  7  5  3  1 (paperback)
2  4  6  8  10  9  7  5  3  1 (hardcover)

*For Georgina,*
*who makes the music in my heart*

# Contents

# Angus MacMouse Brings Down the House

# It's a Rat!

Angus MacMouse was all alone in the world, living in a narrow back alley in Brooklyn, New York, and scavenging for a meager meal wherever he could. Every day was a struggle to avoid prowling cats, trash trucks, tramping feet, rat poison, mousetraps, bad weather, nasty rats who stole his food, and other perils. Every night as he curled up in his nest of string and rags, he hoped desperately that something might happen—something wonderful and magical—that would change his unhappy life forever.

One dreary night something did happen.

Angus had spent a long, damp, miserable evening huddled in the rain behind a trash can that oozed a foul-smelling liquid. He was trapped there by a scrawny orange cat. The hungry cat had surprised him, pounced on him, and nearly had him for dinner. Angus was wet and slippery from the rain, and the cat had lost her grip on his skinny tail. But the cat did not give up her meal so easily and chased Angus, zigzagging wildly down the alley until he darted into the narrow space behind the garbage can, his heart pounding in terror.

Then the waiting had begun. He heard the cat softly creeping through the puddles around the trash can . . . back and forth, back and forth. Sometimes he caught a glimpse of frightening golden eyes peering at him, and then a paw would dart into the narrow space, slashing and scratching, trying to grab the tender brown mouse with razor-like claws.

At last, not liking the cold rain, the cat grew impatient and gave up the hunt. She hissed angrily and wandered away to find an easier meal. Still, Angus waited. He had known cats who were clever enough to come back just in time to catch an unsuspecting mouse as he was about to make his escape. But Angus knew all their tricks. Finally, he peeped out, his dark eyes shining and his nose quivering as he cautiously sniffed the night air. The cat was gone.

Angus crept out of his hiding place. He shivered and pulled his threadbare coat around his shoulders. Now that the danger was past, he remembered how hungry he was. He hadn't eaten anything for two days except a soggy crust of bread and a rotted apple core. Staying close to the brick walls of the buildings, he scampered along the alleyway searching for something to eat. There was a diner nearby that might have some tasty crumbs to offer, but the rats there were mean and selfish. He hurried along his way, stopping often to sniff the air for lurking cats.

*Why does life have to be so difficult?* he thought in despair.

Just then, something in the damp, dark alley made his ears prick up and his whiskers tremble. It was heavenly music floating through the air. Even with his sensitive ears he could barely hear it above the sound of the pelting rain, but as he scurried down the alley it got a little louder. Where could it be coming from? Desperate not to let it slip away, he stopped again to listen. Then, his ears tingling, he ran faster and faster, following the magical sound until he came to a dirty cellar window. A dim light shone through the grimy glass. In one corner the glass was cracked and a piece was missing, making a perfect mouse-size hole. Angus squeezed through.

Inside the cellar, the music grew louder, and Angus followed the sound as if he were tracking down the finest piece of aged cheese. But his excitement made him forget how hungry he was; nothing mattered now except the beautiful music. He had to find where it was coming from. He had to get as close to it as he could. Nothing he had ever known in his short, dismal life was so glorious or thrilling.

He climbed over boxes and crates. He scrambled over piles of rope. He sneezed when he tripped over some dusty old programs. He wandered past racks of colorful costumes and a whole forest of painted trees. All the while, the music kept getting louder until, finally, it was so loud it made his ears twitch, and he could feel the floor vibrate beneath his feet. A bright beam of light fell on him from above. Angus looked up. The light was coming from a crack that outlined a trapdoor in the ceiling. A long rope dangled from it. The music was up there, he was sure of it! Eagerly, he climbed up the rope toward the light—and the music.

Angus slipped through the crack and stood in the middle of the stage of the old Brooklyn Opera House, his mouth open in awe, his tail quivering. Never had he seen anything so spectacular. Stunned, he let a faint *squeak!* escape his lips.

Brilliant lights illuminated the stage from every direction. He could feel their heat on his wet fur. Dozens of people dressed in elaborate costumes moved about, singing a rousing chorus. Angus felt giddy. He was surrounded by a sea of light, and color, and motion, and sound.

Suddenly, the chorus ended, the music became very quiet, and a spotlight beamed down on a dark-haired woman as she swept onto the stage. It was Minnie McGraw, the great soprano! Angus remembered seeing her picture on posters outside the opera house. There was a roar of applause from the audience as she moved to the center of the stage. Her enormous gown almost knocked him over as she walked past. Then she stretched out her plump arms, took a deep breath, and began to sing. The music from the orchestra soared and Minnie's magnificent voice soared with it. Angus felt his heart pound in his chest as the music engulfed him and filled the opera house right up to the rafters.

He turned around, and beyond the glare of the footlights, he saw the orchestra. The trumpets, flutes, and trombones gleamed. The violinists' bows went up and down, up and down, as if they were dancing. A man beat an enormous drum that made a sound like thunder. Another man, a very important-looking man wearing a black tuxedo, waved a white stick in the air. All the musicians watched him as they played. The man with the stick reminded Angus of the policeman on the corner who directed traffic. The policeman made the cars stop and go, and it seemed that the man in the tuxedo made the music stop and go. He made it get loud or soft, fast or slow, happy or sad. He was the man in charge of making the music.

Angus had a thrilling thought: *If I had a little white stick, I could make music too.*

Then . . . it happened.

Minnie McGraw was reaching the end of her aria when she looked down and saw Angus standing quietly in the middle of the stage. Her face twisted in horror. She did not scream exactly, but her famous soprano voice kept getting higher, and higher, and *higher*, until she hit a note that no human being had ever hit before. A crackling noise came from the ceiling of the opera house, and every eye turned to look at the enormous crystal chandelier that hung over their heads. The orchestra stopped playing. The audience

gasped. Then they heard a tinkling sound as thousands of crystals shattered and fell to the floor like glittering rain.

Some people cowered and screamed. Others clapped and cheered. Some yelled, "Bravo! Bravo!"

Minnie McGraw nearly fainted. She collapsed on the stage and began fanning herself.

Angus was confused and frightened. Had he done something wrong? As the audience rushed to leave, the huge velvet curtain came down with a thud. Everyone onstage gathered around him. They all looked very upset.

"Aach! It's a rat!"

"Oh, he's horrible. Filthy creature!"

"Look at those beady eyes."

"And that ugly tail."

"He ruined the opera!"

"Troublemaker!"

"Ne'er-do-well!"

Through the angry crowd a sweet voice called, "Wait! Don't hurt him!"

A beautiful girl pushed her way into the tight circle that surrounded Angus. She smiled as she reached down and gently scooped him up in her hand.

"You're frightening him. He's not a dirty rat. He's just a dear little mouse. Look . . . he's shaking. Poor little fellow."

"Throw him out in the alley where he belongs," said the baritone.

"Feed him to the cat!" cried the tenor.

There was a murmur of agreement from the chorus. The beautiful golden-haired girl looked worried for a moment, but then her face brightened.

"Daddy!" she cried, as a short, round man with a long mustache came huffing and puffing onto the stage from the wings.

"I saw the whole thing!" he panted. "It was absolutely incredible! What a stroke of luck!" He glanced over at Minnie, who was still slumped on the stage, her dress billowing around her like a soft, pink cloud.

"Minnie, darling," he said, "you were marvelous! Stupendous! People will be talking about this for years!"

"Daddy?"

"Not now, Rosemary! We've got to find that rat."

"Daddy?"

"Rosemary, please! Daddy is very busy."

"But, Daddy, look. I have him right here in my hand. Isn't he the sweetest thing? Can I keep him?"

Rosemary held out her hand and Angus, feeling quite comfortable and safe there, decided to tidy himself up a bit and began washing his whiskers with his paws.

Mortimer Brimley looked at Angus. His eyes grew large and the ends of his mustache wiggled as he smiled. He was not looking at a small mouse. He was looking at a huge opportunity.

# Mortimer's Plan

Angus watched as Mortimer Brimley paced back and forth on the stage, muttering to himself while he preened his perfectly waxed mustache. Every once in a while he stopped his pacing, looked at Minnie, then looked at Angus, stroked his mustache, and said, "Hmmmm...."

In the wings, the cast and crew huddled in little groups, whispering to each other. Chorus members, wearing their colorful costumes, relaxed on the stage while they waited for Mortimer. After ten minutes of pacing, gesturing, and muttering, he suddenly clapped his hands together with a startling smack. Angus trembled, and even Rosemary jumped.

"Attention! Attention, everyone!" shouted Mortimer. The performers gathered around him. Taking a deep breath so he looked even rounder than before, he said, "Ladies and gentlemen! This is the big break our little company has been waiting for, and we must seize the moment. So here is what we are going to do. We are going on a wor-r-rld tour-r-r!" he announced, rolling his *r*'s with gusto. When he was excited, Mortimer's Scottish brogue became more pronounced. "Aye, a world tour, Minnie. Just think of it! The whole wor-r-rld will want to hear you hit the high note that no soprano has ever hit before—the note that shattered the chandelier in the Brooklyn Opera House. We'll go to London, Paris, and Rome. Three weeks in every city should suffice. And finally, we'll come home in triumph to New York!"

Mortimer helped Minnie get to her feet and began brushing her off. "Didn't I always tell you I'd get you to the Metropolitan someday? This is our big opportunity!"

Minnie was still shaken and upset. "B-b-but Mortimer," she stammered, "I—I don't think I can do it. I was terrified by that awful mouse. You know how I hate mice. I'll never be able to hit that note again."

Mortimer put his arm around Minnie, gave her a gentle squeeze, and with a voice as soft as velvet he said, "Ah, Minnie, darling, you must trust your manager. Hasn't Morty always taken good care of you? Don't worry, I've thought of everything. Of course you can hit that note again. And again, and again! All we need is that mouse."

"Oh no, Morty, please! I can't stand the little creatures," Minnie pleaded. But it was no use. When it came to her career, Mortimer always got his way.

He stroked his mustache again with satisfaction, and smoothed the lapels of his finely tailored suit. "I have it all worked out. You see, every performance must be a surprise. No one will know when it's going to happen. Minnie, you will be singing your lovely little heart out. The audience will be thrilled by every magnificent note. We'll let the mouse loose on the stage sometime during the performance—but no one will know when. The audience will be on the edge of their seats! And Minnie, here's the trick—you won't know when it's going to happen either. I guarantee you will hit that high note every time! Trust me, the audience will *love* it!"

He pointed a stout finger at his daughter. "Rosemary! You're in charge of the wee mouse. Don't let anything happen to him. He's our ticket to fame and fortune."

"Don't worry, Daddy. I'll take very good care of him," said Rosemary, still holding Angus in her hand.

"Morty, please . . . ," Minnie began, her cheeks flushed and her chin trembling. But Mortimer was already rushing off to his office to make preparations.

❧

Rosemary had a small, cheerful room, with a narrow bed and a small window that looked out over the street below. Tucked in one corner of the room was a lovely Victorian dollhouse.

When she brought Angus home late that night, she set him down in the neatly furnished parlor. Without wasting any time he ran upstairs and downstairs, carefully sniffing everything as he inspected each charming little room. He decided immediately that this was by far the most wonderful house he had ever seen.

"I hope you'll be comfortable in my dollhouse. I'm twelve now, so I hardly play with it anymore—but it's much too pretty to put up in the attic," said Rosemary as she plumped the tiny pillows on the little bed. She smiled at Angus. "It's the perfect size for you. Now make yourself at home, and I'll go find you some food."

Food! Angus was starving. But he was exhausted too. He climbed up the stairs to the bedroom and curled up on the soft canopy bed. He thought he would just rest there while he waited for Rosemary to return. Maybe she would bring him some cake, or some biscuits, or . . .

Angus drifted off into a deep, peaceful sleep.

Something amazing and wonderful was happening. Minnie McGraw was singing and Angus was conducting the orchestra. He stood on the podium next to the important-looking man. They were both wearing black tuxedos, and Angus had a little white stick that he waved around with great authority. When he pointed at the violinists, they played more furiously. When he slowed down, all the musicians slowed down too. Angus was making the music, and it sounded magnificent. The important-looking man lifted him up and the audience burst into wild applause. Angus bowed again and again as the audience cheered.

But something was not quite right. Why was Minnie still singing?

Angus opened his eyes and realized, to his great disappointment, that he had been dreaming. The roar was not applause at all; it was a garbage truck lumbering down the street. And the singing ... where was the singing coming from?

Angus looked around Rosemary's room. The early morning sun was streaming through the white lace curtains. Rosemary's empty bed was rumpled; her nightgown and robe lay in a heap on the floor. The door was open and the singing seemed to be coming from somewhere down the hall. He recognized the melody of the aria that Minnie McGraw had sung the night before. The voice was similar to Minnie's, but more sweet and sunny, like a summer morning.

*How beautiful,* he thought as he yawned and stretched. *It must be a radio.*

*Sniff! Sniff!* His nose twitched as he detected the tantalizing smell of ripe cheese. He leaped from the bed and scurried down the miniature stairs into the dollhouse kitchen. On the table Rosemary had left him a fine slice of English cheddar, some sunflower seeds, and a dish of fresh water. Angus sat down quickly and ate every bite.

He was washing his whiskers when Rosemary danced into her room, singing Minnie's aria in a beautiful, clear voice. Angus stared at her, his mouth open in surprise. It wasn't the radio after all. Rosemary could sing.

"Ah, there you are!" Rosemary said cheerfully. "Awake at last. And I see you enjoyed your breakfast too." She sat down on her bed and looked at the newspaper she held in her hand. "Well, Daddy was right. Minnie's incredible high note last night has caused quite a sensation. He's busy right now making all the arrangements. I hope you like to travel, little mouse, because we are going on tour."

# In Rosemary's Room

The Brimley house was small and cramped, but to Angus it was heaven. He was warm and dry, there were no hungry cats to chase him, and his new friend, Rosemary, was kind and thoughtful.

Mortimer was rarely at home. He went to work at the opera house every day and Rosemary often went with him. "Taking good care of the mouse" meant that wherever she went she brought Angus along too, carefully carrying him in a small, soft purse.

Rosemary loved to be around the stage and the performers, and she helped out whenever she could with small jobs, whether it was painting scenery or mending costumes. Everyone in the company knew her and tried to look out for her—not because they had to, but because they liked her.

Every time they went to the opera house, Angus hoped that he would hear the beautiful music again. But day after day he didn't see the orchestra or the man in the tuxedo. Sometimes a lady came and played the piano so the singers could practice, but it wasn't as grand.

Angus was disappointed, but the buzz of activity was always exciting. He found out that Mortimer was not only Minnie's manager, he was also something called an "impresario." Angus wasn't sure what that meant, but he could see that Mortimer was in charge of almost everything. Perhaps the hardest part of Mortimer's job was keeping Minnie McGraw happy.

"Don't worry, I've thought of everything," said Mortimer at least ten times every day as he prepared the opera company to go on their world tour. But his pampered star was upset. Often, she refused to come out of her dressing room.

She fretted about her high note. "I'll never be able to hit it again! The audience will be disappointed and angry. What if they hiss and boo? What if they want their money back?"

She worried about seeing Angus. "I never want to see that hideous creature again. He frightens me. Get rid of him! I hate him, hate him, *hate him*!"

She complained about her nerves. "I won't be able to sing a note, I just know it. I'm too frazzled!"

Mortimer always knew how to calm her down. He brought her flowers and chocolates, and told her how famous she would be. He patted her soft, white hand and told her that her fans would love and adore her more than ever. Minnie liked to hear how much her fans loved her. By the time Mortimer was finished, Minnie was so relaxed she was practically purring. Then he could coax her out of her dressing room for rehearsals.

Unfortunately, it never lasted very long. By the next day she was jittery and nervous all over again.

While Mortimer was busy making plans and preparations, Angus was getting quite comfortable in

Rosemary's dollhouse. His life had never been better. Rosemary brought him delicious meals. For breakfast he had bits of rich ginger scone with butter and jam, and tiny sandwiches for lunch. He learned to drink tea with milk and sugar, just like Rosemary. And for supper there was always a lovely piece of cheese and his favorite sunflower seeds. Sometimes they ate together sitting on the floor of Rosemary's little room. Her soft voice and gentle ways made Angus feel safe and comfortable, and when they were finished eating he often crawled into her pocket, curled up, and took a nap. They were quickly becoming good friends, and in their quiet moments alone in her room, Rosemary began to tell Angus her secrets.

"My mother was a great singer like Minnie McGraw, you know," she told him. "Daddy was her manager too. She performed all over the world and I used to travel with them everywhere. I loved sitting in the front row and watching her rehearse. When I was eight we were in Italy when Mother suddenly got very sick. The doctors couldn't save her. Poor Daddy . . . his heart was broken. We came home and Daddy wouldn't even listen to music for almost two years. Then he heard about a soprano named Minnie McGraw. She's Scottish like Daddy, so he took an interest in her. Someone convinced him to go hear her sing, and ever since then all he seems to care about is Minnie and her career. Sometimes I think it's just his way of forgetting how much he misses Mother."

Tears welled up in Rosemary's eyes. "I miss her too," she said, her voice trembling. "Daddy is always so busy now. I wish we could just sit and talk like we used to. I want to tell him how much I want singing lessons, but he hates it when I sing."

Rosemary tickled Angus's ears. "Daddy will never take me seriously, especially when he's managing the career of a great singer like Minnie McGraw. All I hear is, 'Minnie this, and Minnie that, and isn't Minnie wonderful?' Or, 'Not now, Rosemary. I'm too busy, Rosemary.' He thinks I'm being childish. He doesn't even see that I'm growing up."

She tried to wipe away her tears. It made Angus's heart ache to see his best friend so sad and lonely. He tried to cheer her up. He ran up her arm and across her shoulder, crawled under her golden hair and nuzzled the back of her neck.

"Oh, stop! Stop! Your whiskers tickle!" she cried. Then Rosemary rolled over on the floor squealing with laughter, and Angus was glad he'd made her happy, if only for a moment.

# Harriet to the Rescue

In a few weeks everything was ready. The company had rehearsed their production of Bizet's opera *Carmen* to perfection. The costumes were packed away in trunks, the scenery was crated up, transportation was arranged, and hotels were booked for the cast and crew.

A specially made leather trunk from France was delivered to the Brimley house. When the shiny brass latches were undone, the top lifted up, the front opened, and Rosemary's dollhouse fit inside perfectly. All the furniture was glued down, or secured with tiny screws, to keep it from shifting. And air holes had been drilled in the sides of the trunk so Angus could breathe when the opera company was traveling from city to city.

"You see, I have thought of everything!" said Rosemary's father proudly, as he demonstrated how the new trunk worked, and snapped the latches shut.

Angus curled up on his little bed in the darkness. He didn't mind knowing he was locked inside the trunk. He felt safe and comfortable as long as he could see Rosemary through one of the peepholes.

"Don't worry," she whispered. "I'll be right here with you the whole time."

&

The first stop on the world tour was London. The opera company landed in England late at night and took a train to Victoria Station, where a large crowd of people and reporters rushed to meet them. It seemed everyone was anxious to catch a glimpse of Minnie McGraw, who some were already calling "the greatest soprano that ever lived." People shouted and cameras flashed. Mortimer had made sure a limousine was waiting to whisk Minnie to the hotel. He hurried Minnie through the crowds and into the car, then he climbed in and slammed the door. They sped away.

Rosemary, Angus, and the rest of the company were left behind, standing at the curb in a soft, drizzling rain. A long row of shiny black taxis waited for them. Harriet Underwood, the wardrobe mistress, popped up her umbrella and put a reassuring arm around Rosemary's shoulders. "Don't worry, my dear," she said. "Your father has a lot on his mind these days. I'll look after you."

&#x6A1;&#x9;

In just a few days, the production was ready. The sets were constructed, the costumes and props were unpacked, and the performers had settled into their new dressing rooms. Unfortunately, Mortimer Brimley had not thought of *everything*. He had forgotten one very important detail.

The opera company was rehearsing on the afternoon of their first London performance. Mortimer was showing Rosemary what he wanted her to do when she released Angus onto the stage. She would play a peasant girl in the opera, and

Harriet had made her a costume to wear with a special pocket sewn into the apron so Angus could remain hidden until it was time to let him loose.

"I want you to blend in with the chorus," said Mortimer. "Don't do anything to draw attention to yourself. And try not to let Minnie see you, either. Remember, Rosemary, we need this to be a big surprise."

Angus peeked out of the secret pocket and looked around the stage. It looked very much like the Brooklyn Opera House with all the lights, dangling ropes, and heavy velvet curtains. Beyond the stage and the orchestra pit, the darkened theater looked huge and cavernous with row upon row of plush red seats, and tiers of balconies decorated with ornate carvings painted in gold. It even had an enormous chandelier. Angus stared at the chandelier, its crystals twinkling in the darkness. Suddenly, his mouth dropped open and he looked up at Rosemary. She, too, was staring into the empty theater and up at the ceiling. He knew she was thinking the same dreadful thought.

"Um . . . Daddy?"

"What? Do I have to repeat everything again? I knew you weren't listening!"

"I was listening. But...I think there is a problem."

Mortimer looked surprised, then angry. "A problem? There *ar-r-re* no problems!" he sputtered in his heavy Scottish accent. "Your job is to look after the wee mouse. You're not here to tell your father there is a problem!"

Rosemary summoned her courage and blurted out her fear. "The chandelier! If Minnie hits her high note, she'll shatter the chandelier again. We can't have her breaking things wherever we go . . . can we, Daddy?"

Mortimer turned a deep shade of red. He began pacing back and forth across the stage, nervously wringing his hands. "The chandelier . . . the chandelier . . . ," he muttered over and over. Finally, he stopped pacing and announced, "There is no such thing as a problem that cannot be solved. Harriet! I need Harriet! Where is she?"

Then Mortimer did something quite surprising. He leaned over and kissed Rosemary on her forehead. "Well done, Rosie."

He patted his daughter on the head like she was a puppy, then he rushed off, still bellowing for Harriet. Rosemary looked down at Angus and they both smiled.

The rest of the day was a blur of activity. Lighting was adjusted and final touches were put on the scenery. Harriet and a team of seamstresses worked feverishly to create a huge red velvet pouch that was padded with layer upon layer of cotton. When it was finished, workmen hoisted it carefully up to the ceiling so it surrounded the delicate crystals of the magnificent chandelier. Then, heavy silken drawstrings at the top of the pouch were pulled tight so the chandelier was completely enclosed.

With only an hour left before the curtain rose for the opening performance, Mortimer, Harriet, and Rosemary stood on the stage and looked up at what appeared to be a giant red cocoon suspended from the ceiling.

Mortimer mopped his brow. "I think it will work," he said.

"I'm sure it will work, sir," said Harriet, smiling proudly at her creation.

"Of course it will," chimed in Rosemary.

"Thank you both for your help. Everything is under control now," said Mortimer with a sigh of relief. "Rosemary, are you and the mouse ready? He understands what he needs to do?"

She looked down at Angus. He was resting comfortably in her apron pocket. Now and then he peeked out to observe everything with his large, brown eyes.

Rosemary smiled and nodded. "We're ready."

"Excellent! Then, on with the show!" exclaimed Mortimer, twirling his mustache with satisfaction.

# Opening Night

A strange feeling of calm settled upon everyone backstage that night at the London Opera House. The usual excited chatter before a performance had vanished; if anyone spoke it was in a whisper. There was no hustle or bustle, no last-minute panic to fix this or that. Mortimer was right—everything was under control. People stood quietly in the wings, waiting in hushed anticipation for the curtain to go up on what might be the greatest performance of their lives.

Or—it could turn out to be a crushing disaster. Everything was riding on Minnie McGraw, and on a little mouse being able to make her hit that incredible note.

Angus poked his head out of Rosemary's pocket just as the musicians in the orchestra took their seats and began to tune their instruments. They created a delightful jumble of sounds, from the high peal of the piccolo to the low rumble of the kettledrum. It made his ears tingle. He was anxious for the curtain to go up so he could see the important-looking man again, and watch him as he waved the white stick that made the music happen.

Angus was not the least bit nervous about the part he had to play. All he had to do was run in front of Minnie and frighten her like he did before. It didn't seem very difficult, but Rosemary had rehearsed with him over and over again what to do. All that mattered to him was that he did his job well and made her happy.

Suddenly, Mortimer appeared in the wings. He had been in Minnie's dressing room for the last hour, preparing her for the performance. He looked tired, but he silently gave everyone an encouraging thumbs-up signal. Minnie was ready. Then he nodded to two stagehands who were dressed entirely in black.

Backstage, all eyes turned to the men in black as they went behind a small curtain and wheeled out a table draped in ruby-colored silk. The musicians finished tuning their instruments and the audience fell silent. Mortimer waited one more minute to let the anticipation build, then he nodded again to the two men. The heavy velvet curtain was drawn back just enough so the two men could slowly wheel the mysterious table over to a corner of the stage; then a spotlight came on, bathing them in a circle of light. The audience murmured as everyone wondered what was happening. Then they gasped as the two men—ever so carefully—lifted the silk shroud to reveal a pyramid, four feet high, of delicate champagne glasses. They sparkled and glittered like jewels beneath the bright lights.

The audience began to applaud when they understood the purpose of the towering champagne glasses. They had bought their tickets to hear the renowned soprano, and now they realized they might actually see her break the glass pyramid with her voice. Would the champagne glasses be shattered into smithereens in one spectacular operatic moment? Or would everyone go home in disappointment? Some people began to chant Minnie's name. The vast theater resounded with "Min-nie! Min-nie! Min-nie!"

Behind the curtain, Mortimer beamed with pride and excitement as he looked around from face to face. Everyone was there except his star, who was still in her dressing room, warming up her voice. He rubbed his hands together with delight.

"This is it, everyone. This is what we have been waiting for and working for. Let's all give our very best and make it a night to remember. With a little luck we'll make history tonight!"

The two stagehands returned and got ready to raise the curtain. In a moment, a roar of applause rose from the audience. Angus wondered what was happening and looked up at Rosemary.

"That must be the conductor coming to the podium," she whispered.

Together they peeked out from the wings just in time to see the important-looking man take a bow, then turn around and face the orchestra. He looked very serious as he raised his arms into the air. He held the white stick motionless above his head. He paused. The musicians waited and watched. The instant the white stick moved, the violinists' bows began to dance up and down, the trumpeters and clarinetists blew, and fingers flew over the keys of flutes, oboes, and bassoons.

The rousing tempo pounded, the percussionist crashed his cymbals again and again, and the conductor's stick became a white blur of motion. Angus felt his heart swell in his chest as the glorious music of the overture swept over him. Rosemary reached down and stroked his forehead, her fingers trembling with excitement. They watched the orchestra play as if they were in a dream, carried away by the wonderful music. Rosemary hummed the beautiful melodies and Angus waved his arm, copying the conductor's movements exactly. They both sighed when the last notes of the overture faded away.

The audience applauded as the curtain rose slowly on a charming village scene.

Mortimer had chosen the opera *Carmen* because it was one of Minnie's best roles, and because there were so many scenes where Minnie was onstage with the chorus. There was even a children's chorus, so Rosemary would not be too obvious. Mortimer would have lots of opportunities to give her the signal to let Angus loose.

As the stage filled with people singing the first lilting chorus, Rosemary explained the story to Angus. "You see? It's a little town square in Spain. On one side of the square is a factory, and on the other is a guardhouse. The soldiers are singing about the townspeople, and the pretty factory girls as they pass by. Soon we'll see Minnie come onstage. She plays Carmen, a gypsy girl who works in the factory. She's a little wild and a little dangerous. She teases the tenor, Don José, who is one of the soldiers. He's bewitched by her and falls madly in love. But, a little later, Carmen falls in love with the bullfighter, Escamillo. Of course, Don José becomes jealous. Then things get . . . well . . . a bit nasty."

Angus watched, fascinated, as the scenes unfolded before them and the performers acted out the passionate drama. He watched the conductor, too, as he used his white stick to make the music tell the story. Most of the songs were gay and lively, but again and again Angus heard strains of a darker melody, like fire flickering through

some of the scenes. Rosemary warned him that just before the final curtain, the tension would build into a violent encounter between Carmen and Don José.

Every member of the company was performing their best, and Minnie's voice was spectacular. Every time she came onstage, or finished one of her songs, the audience went wild for her, applauding and cheering.

Rosemary and Angus waited, hidden in the wings. She kept looking at her father, watching for the signal, but Mortimer was taking his time, letting the suspense build. They waited and waited. By the middle of the second act, Rosemary started to fidget.

The handsome Italian tenor, Carlo Grimaldi, sang the haunting "Flower Song," Don José's emotional aria about a flower Carmen gave to him which he had kept and cherished. The audience loved him. They shouted, "Bravo! Bravo!" and a few flowers flew through the air. Carlo bowed with a grand flourish; then he strutted to center stage, scooped up a rose and, in an elegant gesture, bowed to Minnie and presented it to her. She clutched it to her breast and the audience cheered for them in delight. Rosemary and Angus couldn't help but smile—everything about this night was so exciting.

Rosemary sighed and nervously fussed with her costume. Angus knew she was anxious to be onstage with the other performers. This was a night she had dreamed of—her very first performance in an opera. Still, Mortimer kept them waiting impatiently through the entire third act.

The audience fell into a respectful silence as Act Four opened. The orchestra played the prelude to the final scene with its flashing Spanish rhythms and jangling tambourines. There was a burst of applause as the curtain rose on a colorful, festive square outside the bullring in Seville. Street hawkers selling oranges and fans, townspeople, soldiers, aristocrats, and peasants were all awaiting a grand procession into the arena. The children's chorus merrily ran onstage, singing excitedly about the coming parade of town officials and bullfighters.

At last, Mortimer casually walked over to Rosemary and touched her shoulder. He bent over and whispered in her ear, "Go ahead now, Rosie. Remember everything I told you. Blend in. Keep an eye on me . . . watch for my signal."

He gave his daughter a little push, and she and Angus emerged into the bright, hot lights of the stage.

"Here we go!" she whispered. She took a deep breath and began to weave in and out of the crowd, swaying with the music. Angus had to hold on tightly in the apron pocket as her dress swirled around her legs.

Rosemary cheered along with the children's chorus as the procession began. Harriet Underwood had created fabulous costumes for the team of bullfighters, or *toreros,* with sparkling beads and colorful embroidery. And Mortimer had arranged for two magnificent black horses to carry the picadors across the stage. The glittering spectacle was breathtaking.

Moments later, a thunderous shout from the chorus announced the arrival of their hero. As the crowd began to sing the "Toreador Song," Escamillo made his dramatic entrance with Carmen on his arm. A spotlight beamed down from above and followed them around the stage. It was all so thrilling, Angus felt he had to peek out and steal a look. Cautiously, he poked his head out of the pocket. There was Minnie, looking exactly the way a great soprano should look. Her gown of red satin and black lace was splendid, her dark curls cascaded down onto her bare shoulders, and her cheeks were flushed from the heat of the lights. But Angus thought he saw something else too. A peculiar look glimmered in her eyes. Was it a hint of panic?

*Why is she frightened of me?* he wondered. *She's so big, and I'm so small.* Still, he felt a pang of sympathy for her. Not long ago, fear had been his constant companion. Living in the alleyways of Brooklyn, he was frightened all the time: afraid of cats and rats and mousetraps, afraid of hunger, afraid of being alone. He shuddered and hoped he would never have that horrible feeling again.

Minnie and Giulio Gatto, the baritone who played Escamillo, began to sing a duet, their glorious voices ringing out, filling the opera house all the way up to the highest balconies.

At that moment, something unexpected happened that nearly ruined all of Mortimer Brimley's carefully made plans. Someone on the crowded stage bumped into Rosemary and made her stumble. When she stumbled her shoe caught in the hem of her long peasant dress and the material tore with a loud *rrrrrrip!* She lost her balance and lurched forward, about to fall headlong onto the stage. Two ladies in the chorus grabbed her and yanked her up just in time, but their sudden reaction caused Rosemary's apron to flip up violently. Angus was catapulted out of the pocket and into the air.

Rosemary gasped and tried to catch him, but he was hurtling along too fast. Angus squealed and did the only thing he could think of—he tucked himself into a little ball. He landed with a *plop* on the stage and rolled between dozens of tramping feet. Miraculously, no one stepped on him. He got up dazed and bewildered, and immediately did what all mice do when they are frightened—he ran as fast as he could! He ran first in one direction and saw Mortimer standing in the wings frantically waving his arms, so he turned around and darted in the other direction, back toward Rosemary. She was waving her arms in alarm too. What was he to do? She pointed desperately in the direction of Minnie McGraw. Angus suddenly remembered what he had to do.

There was no time to look to Mortimer for the signal, no time for anything. He had to improvise.

Fortunately, Minnie was oblivious to the whole incident. She was standing at center stage, her back to the chorus, singing with all her heart. Angus ran straight for her and leaped onto her dress. He scurried up to her waist, then onto her bodice, and finally scrambled on top of her ample bosom. This was definitely not what he had

rehearsed with Rosemary, but it was the best he could do under the circumstances. He looked Minnie right in the eye and squeaked.

Minnie looked down and saw a mouse three inches from the end of her nose—then reacted exactly as Mortimer had predicted. Instantly, her voice rose to an impossible pitch. Just when it seemed it could not possibly get any higher, it got higher, and then *higher.*

Angus felt her hot, sweet breath on his face, the vibration from her voice made his whiskers hum like telephone wires, and his eardrums felt as though they would burst. Just before he clapped his paws over his ears, he heard another sound. It sounded like the tinkling of thousands of tiny bells. The champagne-glass pyramid was exploding, sending a spectacular display of glittering fragments up into the air like fireworks, then down again onto the stage.

Minnie finally ran out of breath. Her eyes rolled back, her black false eyelashes fluttered, her body went limp, and she began to crumple like a puppet onto the stage. Angus held on tight and fell with her. He leaped off just in time to avoid being crushed.

Minnie lay in a heap of ruffles and ribbons and lace on the stage. Her billowing costume acted like a big pillow for her to fall on; she looked quite comfortable, as though she had just lain down for a nice nap.

Rosemary was right there to scoop Angus up to safety. All she could do was whisper, "Oh, my goodness . . . oh, my goodness . . ." over and over. She kissed him on his nose.

The conductor stopped conducting, the orchestra stopped playing, and the chorus stopped singing. Mortimer stood in the wings, unable to move, his eyes wide, his mouth agape, his hands clutching the lapels of his best black suit. In the audience no one moved a finger or even an eyebrow. Expressions of amazement and disbelief were frozen on every face. But the stunned silence lasted only a moment before pandemonium broke loose. The audience jumped to their feet and roared their approval; they cheered, they whistled, they stamped their feet, and they clapped until their hands hurt. Hats, gloves, and programs flew into the air and rained down from the balconies. Hundreds of flowers were thrown onto the stage until it was littered with a pastel sea of carnations, lilies, and roses.

When the performers onstage finally got their wits about them, they rushed to Minnie's side. Carlo Grimaldi produced some smelling salts and waved them under her nose. Gradually, Minnie revived, and the thunderous sound of the applause gave her the strength to stand up. Carlo gave her his arm for support and helped her to center stage where she made bows and curtsies, and smiled and blew kisses to the grateful audience. People tore up their programs and tossed them into the air like confetti. They threw more flowers. Then Mortimer walked triumphantly onstage, kissed Minnie's hand, and presented her with a huge bouquet of scarlet roses.

The cheering went on and on.

In all its years of fabulous performances, no one could remember a night at the London Opera House quite like this one.

# A Knock at the Door

An hour later, after scrubbing off their makeup and changing into their street clothes, the giddy performers left the opera house and rushed back to the hotel for a lavish celebration.

Mortimer escorted Minnie to a limousine that was waiting for them. He didn't seem to notice that his daughter Rosemary stayed behind. It was late and she and Angus were tired, but they were too excited to go to bed. She decided to remain backstage in the wardrobe room and visit with Harriet Underwood. Harriet always stayed late to look after the costumes, and tonight she needed to repair the tear in Rosemary's dress. They had become good friends, and fortunately, Harriet was very fond of Angus too. She had promised to make him a new suit of clothes.

"This little mouse is the *real* star!" she said as she took out her measuring tape and began to measure his shoulders and arms. "Where would Minnie McGraw be tonight without him? If he is going to be in the opera, he should be properly dressed."

Angus thought it felt nice to be appreciated. He wished he could wrap up that feeling and give it to Rosemary.

While Harriet was busy measuring, a tall man walked into the wardrobe room and quietly sat down on one of the trunks.

"Good evening, ladies," he said, not noticing Angus.

Angus did not recognize him at first. He was wearing an argyle sweater and wire-rimmed glasses perched on his long, thin nose. He had the intelligent, casual appearance of a college professor. He seemed very familiar.

"Charles!" said Harriet, blushing. "You were magnificent tonight, as always. That was quite a performance, wasn't it?"

"It was a great success by any standard," said the man named Charles. "I thought perhaps we could celebrate and go out for a late-night supper. Would you like that?"

"I would love it," Harriet replied. Standing up, she nervously smoothed her hair and tugged at her blue cardigan. "Do I look all right? Perhaps I should change into something more dressy."

Charles smiled. "Nonsense. You look lovely. How about you, Rosemary? Would you like to come along? I think you have earned a little fun."

"I'd like to come, but I have to look after Angus. I should probably take him back to the hotel."

The man got up and peered down at Angus through his glasses. "Oh, I beg your pardon. I didn't see you there," he said, and carefully shook Angus's tiny paw with his thumb and forefinger. "It's a great pleasure to meet you, Angus. Your role in tonight's opera was quite spectacular. I congratulate you. By the way, I'm Charles Hyde-Smith, the conductor."

"We usually just call him 'Maestro,'" said Rosemary.

Angus's jaw dropped. The conductor. Of

course! Angus had not recognized him without his tuxedo.

"Angus loves your music, Maestro," said Rosemary. "I watch him every time the orchestra plays. He loves to watch you conduct and he imitates every move you make. I think he's a musician at heart."

"Well, I'm very honored," said the Maestro.

"Anyone who loves great music is a friend of mine. I think we should *all* go out and celebrate. After all, the evening would have been a resounding flop if not for the brilliant performance of our little friend. Am I right?"

"Absolutely," said Rosemary.

"Those are my thoughts exactly," agreed Harriet.

So, for the first time ever, Angus dined in a fine restaurant where people were polite, and waited on him, and called him "sir." He was careful to wash himself meticulously so he would not get little footprints on the white tablecloth. He had a few nibbles of Rosemary's dinner, and when the Maestro mentioned to the waiter that Angus was one of the stars of the opera, he brought over a small silver tray of the restaurant's finest cheeses. The heady aroma of the Blue Stilton cheese almost made Angus swoon. He even tried a sip of the Maestro's champagne, but the bubbles tickled his nose and made him sneeze. Never in his life had he had such a wonderful night.

After dinner they rode back to the hotel in a taxi, and the Maestro himself carried Angus on the elevator up to their suite. Before he said good night, Charles Hyde-Smith invited Angus and Rosemary to come to his rehearsals any time they wanted. Then he had an even better idea.

"Perhaps I can teach you a little more about the music—and conducting. Would you like that?" he asked.

"Oh yes! We'd love that, wouldn't we?" said Rosemary. Angus nodded enthusiastically.

They said good night, then Charles escorted Harriet to her room down the hall.

Rosemary and Angus went to bed exhausted, but their spirits were soaring as high as Minnie McGraw's spectacular, glass-shattering note.

❧

The headlines in the London papers glowed with praise.

"Famed Soprano Delivers Spectacular Performance"

"Audience Thrilled by 'Shattering' Aria"

"Minnie McGraw Does It Again!"

Mortimer paced around the hotel suite, barely able to contain his excitement. He had not been to bed at all. He was still wearing his rumpled suit from the night before, his hair was tousled, and his mustache was askew. He read passages from the reviews out loud. As soon as he finished reading one, he shouted, "Listen to this one!" and read another and another. Minnie lounged on the sofa, surrounded by satin pillows, flowers, and chocolates, listening intently, basking in the adoring words of the press.

"Oh, Morty, darling, read them again," she sighed, and then stuffed a bonbon in her mouth.

Rosemary sat on the floor nearby, with Angus carefully hidden in her lap so Minnie wouldn't know he was there. Her father had dropped a few of the newspapers on the floor next to her as he finished reading them. Angus yawned as he glanced at the headlines and the pictures. He was still tired from all the excitement of the night before, and he was getting bored listening to Mortimer read the reviews over and over. He busied himself washing his whiskers. He felt quite satisfied with himself. He had done his job well, the performance was a huge success, and everyone was happy. Best of all, the Maestro was going to teach him how to conduct the orchestra. He was tired, but extremely content.

*Can life be any better than this?* he wondered

happily. He curled himself up and closed his eyes for a nap when Rosemary's voice startled him awake.

"Daddy! Did you see this one?" She held up one of the papers for her father to read. She pointed to a short article at the bottom of the page.

Mortimer squinted at it. He read the headline out loud, " 'The Small Secret of Minnie's Success.' Hmmm . . . What's this about?"

He read on:

"Minnie McGraw dazzled the audience last night with her stunning portrayal of Carmen at the London Opera House. But this reviewer was also impressed by the performance of the smallest member of the opera company. He is so small, in fact, I doubt many people even saw him.

"Minnie McGraw's high note last night was nothing less than spectacular, but I am quite certain it would not have been possible without the help of this very talented, intelligent, and fearless member of the cast.

"I saw him plainly from my seat in the second row as he deftly scampered up to Miss

McGraw's . . . ahem . . . nose, and only then was she able to summon up the unearthly note that shattered the towering champagne glasses.

"I shouted 'Bravo' with the rest of the crowd, but I was also cheering for the amazing performance of a little brown mouse . . ."

Mortimer's mouth fell open. "Well, I never! I—I don't believe this!" he stammered.

"Morty? Morty, what is it? Is something wrong?" said Minnie, looking worried.

"I'm not sure . . ."

Mortimer didn't have time to think about the significance of the story. Someone was knocking on the door of their hotel suite.

Rosemary slipped Angus into her pocket and jumped up. "I'll see who it is," she said.

She opened the door and saw a handsome young man with short, dark hair and eyes that sparkled. He had a camera bag slung over his shoulder that was so heavy it made his whole body tilt to one side. He smiled boyishly when he saw Rosemary.

"Hello. Sorry to bother you so early. Well, it's

not all that early, actually, is it? My name is Hendricks. P.J. Hendricks. I'm with the *Daily Herald*," he said. "Um . . . I recognize you from the opera last night, don't I? You're the girl with the mouse . . ."

"Yes, I was there last night. I'm Rosemary Brimley. Can I help you with something?" she asked.

"Well, I was rather hoping you could. Yes, actually . . . you're exactly the person who might be able to help me," said the young man as he fidgeted with his camera bag. "You see, I wrote a little piece for my paper last night, and it seems to have attracted a lot of interest. The telephone has been ringing all morning. People want to know more about that mouse."

Rosemary said, "Oh," and discreetly covered her pocket, and Angus, with her hand.

P.J. Hendricks continued. "It would be fabulous if you could tell me his story. Where did he come from? Did you have to train him? Did he have something to do with the chandelier coming down in Brooklyn? Anything at all would be a huge help."

The young man's brown eyes pleaded. Nevertheless, Rosemary began to shut the door. "I'm sorry, Mr. Hendricks. I don't mean to be rude, but I really can't tell you anything . . ."

"Wait!" cried Mortimer, hurrying over to the door and pushing Rosemary aside. "Just a moment, Mr. Hendricks. I'm Mortimer Brimley, Miss McGraw's manager. If you have any questions, you should talk to me." He quickly tried to smooth his hair and wrinkled clothes. "So, you wrote that piece about the secret of Minnie's success?"

"Yes, that was mine. It's a pleasure to meet you, sir. And congratulations on a spectacular performance. I was just saying I'd like to know more about that mouse I saw last night. I'd love to tell his story in my paper." P.J. Hendricks peered eagerly into the suite as if he were looking for something. "I can see you're busy, and I don't want to be a bother, but I wonder if I could ask you a few questions."

Mortimer glanced over his shoulder at Minnie, who was glowering at them from the sofa. He suddenly seemed impatient with the young man. "Yes, yes, Mr. Hendricks, we'll grant you an interview. But not now. Uh . . . why don't you come back this afternoon? Yes, come for tea. Four o'clock."

"Well, don't expect me to be there," said Minnie, getting up in a huff. "I won't have anything to do with it. I hate that loathsome, filthy creature!" She stormed into her bedroom and slammed the door.

"Don't mind her. She's exhausted, poor darling," said Mortimer.

"Of course, I completely understand. I'll see you later then, Mr. Brimley. Thank you very much. Miss Brimley, it's been a pleasure," said P.J. politely. He grinned as he turned to leave.

Rosemary did not have a chance to answer. Her father abruptly closed the door.

"Well, well, well," he said, rubbing his hands together with obvious pleasure. "It seems our little friend is a very popular fellow all of a sudden. Young Hendricks is onto something that could be big. Really big! I need to think . . . it's always wise to have a plan. Let's get some rest, then this afternoon you can get the mouse cleaned up. Make him look as presentable as possible. Hendricks may want to take some pictures to go with his story."

He bent over and whispered in Rosemary's ear, "Let's not talk about this in front of Minnie. We don't want to upset her. She'll be furious if she thinks she's going to share the spotlight with a mouse."

Then, exhausted, Mortimer wandered off to his room.

Rosemary gently lifted Angus out of her pocket and held him up to her cheek. She liked the feel of his soft fur against her skin. "Did you hear that?" she whispered. "Daddy called you 'our little friend.' He likes you, you know. Not as much as I do, of course, but he likes you."

She walked over to the pile of newspapers on the floor and pulled out the one with P.J. Hendricks's story about Angus at the bottom of the page.

"I think I'll make a scrapbook for you," she said. "I'll cut this out and paste it on the very first page. We'll save every article and every review. If Daddy and Mr. Hendricks have their way, this may be just the beginning. Angus, I think you're going to be a star!"

# The Interview

Angus didn't know exactly what a star was, but the possibility of being more than just a plain brown mouse seemed extremely appealing. He was quite sure Minnie was a star, but he didn't think he could be like her. With his squeaky voice, he couldn't sing a note. Then he wondered if the Maestro was a star. Now *that* was something to be excited about! Angus would be the happiest mouse in the world if he could be like the Maestro. The idea of making the music with a little white stick was so thrilling he had trouble holding still while Rosemary tried to get him ready for their afternoon appointment with P.J. Hendricks.

Angus had a warm, soapy bath in a teacup that Rosemary had borrowed from room service. Then he wiggled and squirmed while she dried him off with a washcloth. With shining fur and half a drop of Mortimer's cologne on his whiskers, he let Rosemary carry him down the hallway to Harriet's room.

"Oh, he looks very handsome, indeed," said Harriet when she opened her door and saw Angus all freshly scrubbed and bathed. Rosemary explained what had happened earlier with the story in the newspaper, the unexpected visit from the young reporter, and the important meeting scheduled for later in the day. She was about to ask Harriet for her help, but she didn't need to.

"Well, I'm very glad you stopped by," said Harriet, immediately grabbing her sewing basket. Harriet was one of those people who was always calm, organized, and prepared for anything. Angus liked that she was neat and tidy too.

"I have a surprise for you," she said, smiling. "I was working on these this morning. Just a few more stitches and they'll be finished." Harriet took two tiny suits out of her basket. One was a stunning black tuxedo with satin lapels and striped pants, and the other was a gray tweed weekend suit with a tartan waistcoat, for more casual occasions. "I think the tweed will be perfect for this afternoon's tea."

Angus desperately wanted to try on the tuxedo, but Harriet put it back in her basket. Rosemary helped him into the gray tweed suit and held him up to look at himself in a large mirror. Angus turned around and around, admiring Harriet's workmanship. The stitches were so tiny they were almost invisible, and the fit was perfect.

"Just a nip and tuck and you'll be done," said Harriet, taking the jacket off Angus for a moment.

Angus was intrigued by the pincushion she always wore on her wrist. It looked like a little cloth tomato stuck with dozens of needles and pins. She took a needle and thread from her pincushion and made the smallest of adjustments, then slipped the jacket back on. She stepped back to look at Angus in his new clothes. "Oh my, that's the finest-looking mouse I've ever seen!" Her voice was full of excitement and just a hint of pride.

"He looks absolutely perfect. Thank you, Harriet." Rosemary paused. "Thank you for everything you've done for me and Angus."

"Oh now! Don't go getting me all teary!" Harriet gave Rosemary a quick hug and shooed them out the door. A moment later she called after them, "Best of luck with the interview this afternoon!"

❦

At four o'clock, a man from room service wheeled a cart covered with crisp white linens into the suite. On the cart were plates of cucumber sandwiches and delicate miniature cakes decorated with tiny frosting flowers, a shining silver tea service, and fine bone china cups and saucers. Two minutes later, P.J. Hendricks knocked on the door.

"Hendricks! Come in," said Mortimer as he shook the young man's hand.

"Good afternoon, Mr. Brimley. Miss Brimley. How nice to see you again," said P.J. with a charming smile. "I've been looking forward to our interview this afternoon. I can't tell you how much I appreciate your taking the time to see me."

Rosemary sat quietly on a chair next to the tea cart. She gave the young man a fleeting smile and a sharp look with her bright blue eyes. Angus peeped cautiously out of her pocket. Rosemary had said not to trust this Hendricks fellow. At least, not yet. He seemed too polite, too friendly, too eager. She said he was a young "go-getter" looking for his big break at the newspaper, and there was no telling what he might do to make a name for himself.

P.J. Hendricks put his bulky camera bag on the floor, settled himself onto the sofa, and looked around the room. "Will Miss McGraw be joining us?" he asked.

"No, I'm afraid not," said Mortimer. "I thought it best to send her off to the beauty parlor for a few hours. It helps her to relax."

"I understand. Absolutely. You're a smart man, Mr. Brimley. That's why I think you will agree we should tell the mouse's story. The public wants to know more about him. Who is he? Where did he come from? How do you get him to scare Miss McGraw into hitting her high note? It's quite obvious he isn't just an ordinary mouse."

Mortimer puffed out his chest and began pacing around the room.

"I agree with you, Hendricks. Aye, it's certainly a story worth telling. Of course, from the moment I saw him, I knew he had potential. He was a starving, wretched little creature when he first appeared in the Brooklyn Opera House. Heaven only knows where he came from. He probably wandered in from a back alley . . . or the gutter. But I could see immediately that he had something special. He stood right in the middle of the stage, oblivious to all the people who might trample him. He didn't even flinch. He was mesmerized by the music, you see. But . . . ," Mortimer paused for a long, theatrical moment, "he almost came to a sudden and tragic end on that very first night! When the chandelier shattered and the performance was ruined, everyone was furious. They were all crying, 'Kill him! Kill the rat!' Can you imagine? They wanted to mur-r-r-der the sweet, harmless, wee fellow. He was just about to get his final 'curtain call.'"

Rosemary had started to pour the tea. As she listened to the colorful story her father was telling, she was so distracted her hand shook, the china clattered, and she nearly dropped a cup and saucer. Mortimer Brimley was giving the public a story they would never forget.

P.J. Hendricks leaned forward. He was scribbling notes in his notebook as fast as he could. "Then what happened?"

"It was my daughter, Rosemary, who saved him from certain death. She scooped him up and held onto him until I arrived to calm everybody down. They have been inseparable ever since."

"This is wonderful . . . wonderful . . . ," said P.J. "May I ask a few questions?"

"Fire away," replied Mortimer, sitting down at last.

"Well, I'd like to call him by name in the story I write. Does he have a name?"

"His name is Angus," said Rosemary. "Angus MacMouse."

"Excellent," said P.J., writing furiously. "Did you give him that name, Miss Brimley?"

"No. That's just his name."

P.J. looked perplexed. He opened his mouth to say something, but then changed his mind. "And, how did you train him to do what he does?"

Rosemary smiled. "Well, Daddy's right. He's a

very smart and special mouse. We didn't have to train him at all. We just asked him. Very politely, of course."

"I see. Fascinating," mused the young reporter, scratching his head with his pencil. "I wonder . . . uh . . . might I meet him? Is that possible? Is he here?"

Mortimer nodded his approval, so Rosemary carefully took Angus out of her pocket and placed him on the tea cart. Angus stretched, and straightened his new clothes; he felt slightly rumpled after being in Rosemary's pocket for so long. He waved to P.J.

The young man leaned forward, his eyes wide with amazement. "He waved to me!" he cried.

"He's very friendly," said Rosemary in a casual tone.

P.J. suddenly seemed less sure of himself. He ran his fingers over his hair.

"Uh . . . can I talk to him?"

"Of course."

P.J. laughed nervously. "I don't know what to say. I mean, I've never interviewed a mouse before!"

"Just be yourself," said Rosemary with a sympathetic smile.

"Be myself. Right. Uh . . . how do you do, Angus? I'm P.J. and I'm extremely pleased to meet you. I don't know what I expected when I came here today, but I didn't expect this . . . I mean, *you*. You're quite an extraordinary fellow!"

Angus was starting to like this young man. He smiled and made the most elegant bow he could. P.J. almost giggled as he groped for his camera bag. "May I take your picture, Angus?"

Mortimer interrupted, "By all means. Take as many pictures as you want, Hendricks."

While P.J. got his camera equipment ready, Rosemary served the tea. She gave Angus a morsel of cake and poured some tea into one of the miniature teacups from her dollhouse. She added a pinch of sugar and a drop of milk so it was just the way he liked it. Angus stirred the tea with the tip of his tail—his only bad habit—and took a sip.

P.J. was amazed and delighted. "He's drinking tea! From a teacup!" he gasped.

He jumped up and began taking pictures: pictures of Angus having tea, pictures of Angus with Rosemary and Mortimer, pictures of Angus posing with one of Minnie's publicity photos. Then Rosemary showed P.J. her dollhouse and the custom-made trunk for traveling. P.J. thought his readers would love it, so he took more pictures of Angus at home in the dollhouse. The flashbulbs popped again and again—so many times that Angus was quite blinded.

After asking a few more questions, P.J. said, "I'd love to stay longer, but I have a deadline to meet. I need to get back to the paper and write my story. Is there anything else you can think of that I should know?"

"Well . . ." Rosemary hesitated, then blurted out the one thing she knew Angus would say if he could. "He would like to conduct the orchestra."

"What? Who wants to conduct? The mouse?" sputtered Mortimer, bewildered.

"Conduct? Really?" exclaimed P.J.

"Yes," said Rosemary. "Every time he watches the Maestro conduct, he imitates him exactly. He's very good. The Maestro has even offered to give him lessons—he says that Angus has a wonderful feel for the music."

"That's ridiculous!" said Mortimer.

"Oh, I wouldn't be too hasty, Mr. Brimley," said P.J., his eyes twinkling. "After what I've seen the last couple of days, I'd say almost anything is possible."

P.J. shook Mortimer's hand and thanked him for the interview. "And thank you, Miss Brimley. You've been very helpful indeed."

Then he carefully shook Angus's tiny paw. "Good-bye, Angus. It's been a great pleasure. I'll do a good job telling your story, I promise." He flashed a quick, brilliant smile and he was gone.

# Angus Takes a Bow

The following night, the performance at the London Opera House was sold out. As the crowd streamed in to take their seats, something seemed different. They were not acting like the usual stuffy audience of proper ladies and gentlemen. They were excited. They were laughing and joking. Strangers were talking with each other.

P.J. Hendricks had written a great story. It took up a full page of the *Daily Herald*, and scattered across the page were some of the delightful pictures he had taken. The public gobbled it up. They were falling in love with the mouse who had gone

"From the Back Alley to the Spotlight." Suddenly, people who had never been to an opera in their lives were clamoring for tickets to see Minnie McGraw and Angus MacMouse in Mortimer Brimley's fantastic production of *Carmen.*

Backstage there was excitement too. The stagehands scurried about adjusting props and scenery. Chorus members huddled in little groups and talked, while Harriet Underwood flitted around checking hems and loose buttons on their costumes. In the dressing rooms the stars were getting dressed and putting on their makeup. Carlo Grimaldi was singing scales, warming up his famous golden tenor voice.

Rosemary waited discreetly in the doorway of Minnie's dressing room. Angus was in her pocket as usual, and together they watched patiently as Mortimer tried to console Minnie. She was sobbing into her lace handkerchief.

"I can't. I can't do it again," she sniffled. "I'm as nervous as a flibbertigibbet just thinking about it."

"You *can* do it, Minnie. I know you can. Just put everything out of your mind except the music. Think about the music."

"I've hit that note twice. Isn't that enough?

Why must I do it at every performance? Mortimer...maybe I could do it without the mouse?"

Mortimer pulled on his mustache. Beads of sweat popped out on his forehead. "Minnie, you know you have tried and tried at rehearsals, and you haven't come even close. Don't think about the mouse. This is a performance like any other. The audience has come to hear you because you are the very best, and they love you. Think of the standing ovations you will get. And the flowers. Think of the reviews!"

Minnie looked at Mortimer and smiled weakly. She began to rally. "You're right, Morty. I work hard every night to give the audience my very best. And they do love me, don't they? I—I can't let them down."

He took her handkerchief and dabbed gently at her eyes. He talked to her and soothed her like she was a little child. "There, that's better. Everything is going to be just fine. It's a full house tonight, and they all came to hear *you* sing. The one and only Minnie McGraw...the greatest soprano who ever lived!"

Rosemary slipped quietly away from the door,

looked down at Angus, and whispered, "I think Minnie's going to be all right. We'd better go get ready."

～ᥫ

The performance that night was brilliant. Minnie, Carlo, and Giulio Gatto, the baritone, sang beautifully, the chorus was lively, and the audience was thrilled. Minnie played Carmen with drama and passion; she'd never sung better. Apparently, frayed nerves did not affect her voice.

Finally, in Act Four, during the crowd scene before the bullfight, Mortimer gave Rosemary the signal. She ducked behind two women in the chorus and carefully set Angus down on the stage. This time everything went according to plan. Angus darted across the stage until he was between Minnie and the footlights, then he jumped up and down to get her attention. There was a slight murmur from the audience when a few people in the front rows saw him. Apparently, Minnie had taken Mortimer's advice—she was too absorbed in her performance to notice the little mouse trying to get her attention.

A moment later she looked down and saw

him; her brown eyes got as big as her favorite chocolate bonbons. Angus felt a twinge of regret, but he knew everyone was depending on him. He gritted his teeth and made a leap for her, pretending he was going to climb up her dress again. The idea that a mouse might be scrambling around on her dress—or *under* her dress—was more than she could bear. Her voice soared up into the stratosphere. The champagne glasses burst into glittering smithereens, and the audience exploded in applause.

This time Minnie did not faint. Clutching her chest with one hand, she staggered backward but didn't collapse. She covered her eyes with her other hand and turned away as she gasped for breath; when she dared to look again, Angus was still standing on the stage in front of her, looking as apologetic as he could. Her face turned crimson and her dark eyes flashed.

"Never again!" she cried as she stormed off the stage.

Rosemary rushed in and picked up Angus. It was dangerous for a small mouse to be surrounded by so many people and so many tramping feet. She was about to put him back in the safety of her pocket, but she changed her mind. Instead, she held him in the palm of her hand so he could look out and see the audience cheering for him. Beyond the bright lights, beyond the orchestra pit and the grinning Maestro, the audience was on its feet, clapping. Among the shouts of "Bravo!" and "Min-nie! Min-nie!" Angus could distinctly hear some people shouting his name. It was incredible.

Standing in Rosemary's hand under the hot lights, with the audience cheering for him, he thought it wouldn't hurt to take a bow. So he did. And then another, and another.

Some people had come prepared with their pockets stuffed with confetti, and now it rained down from the balconies. Flowers began to fly through the air and land on the stage at their feet. Rosemary was bending down to pick up a perfect white rose when someone rushed by, bumping into her, nearly knocking her over. It was Minnie. She stood right in front of them, jealously claiming all the attention for herself.

Rosemary and Angus had their brief moment in the spotlight, and they were happy to slip away quietly into the wings and let Minnie have all the glory. She was, after all, the star. She curtsied with a grand flourish, stooped and gathered up great armloads of flowers from the stage, then blew kisses to the audience. They loved her and cried out for more. After several curtain calls, her spirits were buoyed enough to finish the opera—but just barely. Clearly, she was still shaken and her nerves were rattled. During the last scene, Carlo sometimes had to prop her up, but the enthusiastic applause from the audience kept her going to the end.

Rosemary and Angus peeked out from the wings to watch the finale. In the final scene, Don José and Carmen argue outside the bullring. Amid shouts and fanfare from inside the arena, Don José, in a jealous fury, sings that he won't allow Carmen to cast him aside; it's not too late for them—he still adores her. But Carmen sings that she loves only Escamillo, the toreador. She takes Don José's ring off her finger and flings it to the ground. As the chorus surges out of the arena triumphantly singing the "Toreador Song," Don José lunges at Carmen. His dagger flashes, and with a terrible cry, Carmen falls into his arms.

Playing Carmen's death scene with flair, Minnie finally was able to collapse.

The last dramatic notes were sung, the Maestro rested his baton, the orchestra fell silent, and a thunderous roar went up from the audience. Minnie lay on the stage in an elaborate pose, Carlo loomed over her with his rubber dagger in his hand, and the chorus stood in frozen horror. The curtain slowly came down with a thud.

Rosemary sighed. "Wasn't that thrilling?"

"Listen to the audience!" cried Mortimer as he ran up to them, out of breath and red-faced with excitement. "They loved it! Rosemary, you and Angus were terrific."

"Thank you, Daddy."

"And Minnie! What a trouper!"

The audience was on its feet for the curtain calls, applauding and shouting for the cast. As always, they saved their loudest applause for Minnie, Carlo, and Giulio. But tonight, amid the whistles and "Bravos" there were shouts of "Angus! Angus!"

"Go on out there and take a bow," said Mortimer, smiling.

"What about Minnie? She won't like it."

"Never argue with the audience," he said, and pushed them out onto the stage.

Rosemary quickly stepped up just behind Carlo Grimaldi, where Minnie couldn't see her. The cheering grew louder and louder. Minnie continued to bask in the adoration of the audience, not realizing that she was sharing the applause with the mouse she hated. Carlo, however, turned around and glared at them in disgust. It was a look that said, "What are *you* doing here?" Angus tried to ignore him and, standing on Rosemary's palm, he bowed as elegantly as he could. Rosemary made a dainty curtsy. Then, with the audience still cheering for them, they fled the stage before Minnie noticed them. They were both smiling and giggling when they got back to Mortimer in the wings. He put his arm around his daughter while the three of them watched the final curtain calls.

When the curtain came down for the last time, Mortimer jumped into action. "I have to go congratulate Minnie. Oh, before I forget—P.J. Hendricks is backstage somewhere. He wants to talk to you. He's writing a story for tomorrow's paper, so tell him whatever he needs to know. I'll see you both later."

Mortimer disappeared into the throng of brightly costumed singers. Everyone was smiling and congratulating each other, excited that the performance was a huge success.

༄

Rosemary tried to avoid P.J. Hendricks, in spite of what her father had told her. She headed straight for Harriet's wardrobe room, but P.J. was watching and waiting for her.

"Miss Brimley!" he called. "Wait! I need to talk to you."

Rosemary had to stop and turn around. "Hello, Mr. Hendricks. I read your story in the newspaper. It was very nice."

"Thank you, Miss Brimley. That's what I wanted to talk to you about. Do you have a minute?"

"Well, only a minute. Angus is tired. I need to get him back to the hotel."

P.J. spotted Angus tucked in Rosemary's pocket.

"Angus!" he cried. "You were brilliant tonight. Well done, old chap!"

Angus gave P.J. a friendly wave. He liked P.J. even though Rosemary was still suspicious of him. Animals can sense things about people, and Angus sensed that P.J. was all right.

"I'm doing a follow-up article for my paper. Miss Brimley, I was hoping for your comments on tonight's performance. The response from the audience was incredible. What are your thoughts? Are you excited?"

"Oh, yes. Very." Rosemary waited while P.J. got his pad and pencil ready to take notes. She cleared her throat nervously. Angus knew she was shy, and not at all comfortable with these interviews.

"I . . . um . . . think it went extremely well tonight," she began. "We weren't nervous at all, were we?" Angus shook his head. "We knew what we had to do, and Angus was splendid. All the pressure is on Minnie, really. She is the star. She's the one the audience comes to hear. We just have a small part to play."

"You're being far too modest," said P.J., smiling as he wrote. "You're absolutely essential. Angus— you're getting a lot of fans. Some of them are wondering if it isn't too dangerous out there for you? If I were your size, I'd be scared out of my britches by all those stomping feet. You're not afraid?"

Angus shook his head. *No* . . . he was only afraid of disappointing everyone.

"And what about the schedule? Six performances a week for three weeks is pretty exhausting. So I've been wondering, does Angus have an understudy who can take over for him?"

Rosemary looked offended. "Oh, goodness, no! There's no other mouse who could do what he does. You can see for yourself how special and talented he is."

P.J. apologized. He hadn't meant to upset her. Quickly he changed the subject and asked something about their future performances.

At that moment, Angus stopped paying attention. He was more interested in watching Minnie and Carlo as they walked toward their dressing rooms. Something about them didn't look quite right. They were acting strangely, whispering to each other, and Carlo kept pointing toward them.

Minnie looked more and more upset. Suddenly she burst into tears and buried her face in her hands. Carlo put a consoling arm around her and tried to lead her back to her dressing room. Before they disappeared through the door, Carlo turned and glared at them one more time. Like daggers hitting their mark, Carlo's dark eyes gave Angus a look that made him tremble.

# Caught Napping

For nearly two weeks, Angus had been getting up early to go to the Maestro's suite to have his conducting lessons. For an hour every morning, the Maestro played records on his phonograph, and showed Angus exactly how the conductor made the musicians play the way he wanted them to. Angus had been right—it was a little like a policeman directing traffic.

Charles Hyde-Smith was a strict teacher. Sometimes he made Angus repeat the same passage over and over until he got it right. "Again!" he'd say. "You're in control of the orchestra. Do it again with more authority!"

Six nights a week, Angus went to the opera house and frightened Minnie into hitting her high note. Every performance was getting more and more difficult. Minnie's nerves were so frazzled that sometimes the audience had to wait for her to come onstage. But somehow Mortimer always convinced her to do it "just one more time."

Angus was exhausted. In the afternoons, all he wanted to do was curl up on his little canopy bed and sleep. But at two o'clock on this particular day, Rosemary brought Angus to the opera house where she was meeting Harriet. They wanted to do a little shopping while they were still in London. Rosemary carried Angus up the stairs to the tiny office Mortimer had been using. She knew Angus needed to rest.

As soon as they arrived, Harriet breezed in, looking very stylish in a fitted gray suit. She was carrying her umbrella and pocketbook. "Are we all ready to go?" she inquired.

"Almost," said Rosemary. "I just need to make

Angus comfy while we're gone. He's going to stay here and get some sleep."

While Rosemary arranged a little handkerchief "bed" on the desk, Harriet put on her glasses and peered at Angus with concern. "Oh, you dear little fellow, you *do* look tired." She turned to Rosemary. "I hope he's not working too hard."

"I know . . . he's been very busy, but he loves every bit of it." She put Angus down on Mortimer's desk and waited for him to curl up on the handkerchief. "Now, don't worry. We'll be back in time for tea," she said to him, as they tiptoed out and closed the door.

Angus yawned and closed his eyes. Life with the opera company was exciting, to be sure, but it was very tiring too. A nice nap and then he would feel better. Mortimer was gone for the afternoon, so the office would be quiet. He snuggled into the folds of the handkerchief and began to feel wonderfully sleepy and comfortable. He paid no attention to a noise out in the hallway, but when he heard the doorknob turning he opened one eye.

*Rosemary?* Had she forgotten something?

*Ow!* Angus suddenly felt a sharp pain as something pinched his tail.

Someone was dragging him from his make-shift bed. He tried to grab onto the blotter on Mortimer's desk, but all he could do was clutch frantically at the handkerchief with his toenails. In another moment he was being dangled in the air by his tail. He let the handkerchief go and watched helplessly as it floated down to the floor below. Desperately he struggled and twisted and wiggled. He squeaked as loudly as he could, but it was no use. No one was there to help him. For an instant he saw a gloved hand, then everything became dark. He felt cold metal beneath his feet, and his nose twitched as he detected the pungent odor of . . . tuna fish.

Angus's heart thundered in his chest. He could hear hurried footsteps going down the stairs. He was jostled and bumped in the smelly darkness of the tuna can, and when the can tipped, he slipped back and forth on the oily metal. He heard heavy breathing and more footsteps. A door opened and shut. They stopped moving, and a familiar voice with an Italian accent said triumphantly, "I've got the little vermin!"

Then he heard Minnie's anxious voice. "You have him? Are you sure? Did anyone see you?"

"Don't worry, everything went per-fectly. He's right here. Do you want to see him?"

"Oh, no! Of course not!" cried Min-nie. "Put him right in the cage. Anyway, we shouldn't take any chances. He's very quick, and we can't let him escape."

"Are you sure you don't want to—uh—'dispose' of him?"

"No, no! Not yet, anyway. Just put him in the cage, Carlo. We'll figure out what to do with him later."

The tin can tipped and Angus slid violently to one side, bumping his nose. He heard a mysterious metallic sound, the gloved hand shifted, and he tumbled out, landing with a thump on the bottom of a small wire cage. Moving quickly, Carlo latched the top.

"There!" he said with satisfaction. "The little rat won't escape now."

"He's not a rat, Carlo. He's a mouse."

"*Aach!* Mouse or rat, it doesn't matter. He's a nasty, beady-eyed rodent, and he's caused nothing but trouble. He won't torment you anymore, my darling. You don't need him. You never needed him. Remember who you are—the greatest soprano of all time! Let Mortimer huff and puff. Let him rant and rave. Audiences will still flock to see you. They love *you*, not the wretched little rat."

"I'm still not sure about this. I've worked and trained for so many years—my singing means everything to me. I hope we haven't made a mistake."

Carlo put his arms around Minnie. "Don't worry, my sweet. Soon everyone will forget about the rat, but the whole world will remember that Minnie McGraw sang the highest note *ever*!"

"Oh, Carlo," sighed Minnie, "I hope you're right."

Carlo put the metal cage on the floor and kicked it under his dressing table. "No more trouble from you!" he growled at Angus.

Angus was dazed and bewildered by the suddenness of his mousenapping. He crept into a

corner of the cage and huddled there, trembling
and wondering what would become of him. Carlo
had not taken him very far; he had only carried
him from Mortimer's office, down the stairs to his
dressing room. But Angus felt as though he might
as well be on the far side of the moon. It was a
tiny room, filled with the clutter of a performer:
props, hats, boots, wigs, and scarves. A large trunk
overflowed with Carlo's costumes and souvenirs

of his career. Wilted bouquets had been carelessly tossed on the floor. How would anyone ever find him in this untidy mess? His cage was tucked away in the shadows under the dressing table, obscured by a pile of rumpled clothes.

*Rosemary!* thought Angus, in despair. *Rosemary! Where are you? Please find me—before it's too late.*

He was a pitiful sight. His fur was matted and oily, and he reeked of spoiled fish. Worst of all, the beautiful tweed suit that Harriet had so carefully made for him was stained and ruined. His dismal cage was completely bare, with no food, or water, or bed of any sort. He took off his jacket, carefully laid it out on the grimy floor, and curled up on it. Alone, bruised, and miserable, he closed his eyes and tried to think how he might escape.

# Missing!

When Angus awoke, he was stiff and sore from all his tumbling around in the tuna can. He wrinkled his nose at the strong fishy smell coming from his fur. He had no idea how long he had been asleep. Was it an hour? A day? It wasn't long before he had a clue. The walls of the dressing rooms were thin, so he could plainly hear the musicians in the orchestra tuning up their instruments. He must have slept all afternoon and into the evening. The opera was about to begin.

Suddenly the door opened and Carlo strode in and sat down at his dressing table, his boots just inches from Angus's cage. He put the finishing touches on his stage makeup. As he drew on his black eyebrows and rouged his cheeks, he warmed up his voice by singing scales.

Angus sat and listened. His sensitive ears could hear an astonishing symphony of sounds coming from every corner of the opera house. Air vents between the small dressing rooms made it easy for him to hear Minnie getting ready in the next room. He could hear footsteps racing up and down the corridor, and people talking excitedly outside the door. His ears pricked up when he heard Mortimer's voice coming from Minnie's dressing room.

"Minnie, this is serious. Don't you understand? We have to find that mouse! You won't be able to hit your note. The audience will be disappointed. They've come to hear you . . ."

"Oh, pooh!" Minnie interrupted. "I've been hitting that note night after night. I'm sure I can do it without the help of that nasty little mouse. I don't need him anymore. You'll see, Morty. Everything will be fine."

"You've been listening to Carlo, haven't you? What does he know about anything?" Mortimer sounded angry now. "Who has been helping you and guiding you these last few years? Carlo? No! It was me. I have been taking care of you, making sure you made all the right moves in your career. Now your name will be famous all over the world. What has Carlo ever done for you except try to upstage you? You need to listen to me, Minnie. We need to find that mouse!"

Minnie sniffed. "Carlo cares about me too. I . . . I think he might be in love with me. And he believes in me. He thinks I can hit my note without that horrid mouse."

"I'm sorry to have to say this, Minnie, but I must tell you—not just as your manager, but as your friend—I don't think Carlo cares about anyone but himself. Don't you remember how he always fought with you? Why is he suddenly being so nice? I'll tell you why. He sees your star rising and he wants to ride along with you. The more famous you become, the more acclaim he will get as well. Don't you see?"

There was a long silence in Minnie's dressing room. Angus looked up to see if Carlo had overheard any of the conversation, but his hearing was not as keen as Angus's, and he was too absorbed in adjusting his military costume. Carlo smiled at himself in the mirror, then carefully smoothed his dark, wavy hair.

"No wonder the ladies love me," he muttered to himself.

Suddenly the door burst open and Mortimer rushed in.

"We're in tr-r-rouble!" he said, his excitement exaggerating his brogue. "The wee mouse is missing, and Minnie thinks she can hit her high note without him. We've got to find him. You haven't seen him, have you?"

Carlo pretended to be astonished. "Me? No, Signor Brimley. But if I did, I would crush the little rat beneath my boot! Miss McGraw does not need the rat. She is a prima donna. A star! The audience loves her, not some silly trick she can do."

Mortimer was fuming. The ends of his mustache twitched with rage. "Carlo, you're wrong. Of course the audience loves Minnie. But they have come expecting to hear her hit that note. Audiences don't like to be disappointed. We need to find Angus, and if I find out you had anything to do with his disappearance—your career will be *finished*!"

"Ha!" Carlo sneered.

Angus felt his heart leap. *Rosemary!* She had been standing quietly behind her father, just out of sight. Now he saw her as she stepped into Carlo's dressing room. Her gentle face was red and tear-stained.

"Please, Signor Grimaldi," she pleaded, "please tell us if you know anything about where Angus might be. I'm afraid something awful has happened."

Angus jumped up to the bars of his cage and tried to rattle them as loud as he could. He squeaked and squeaked, but his voice was too tiny to be heard above all the noise coming from the corridor outside the room.

*Rosemary! I'm here!*

Carlo seemed to soften a little at the sight of the heartbroken girl.

"I'm sorry you have lost your little rat, signorina. Perhaps he ran away."

Fresh tears rolled down Rosemary's cheeks. "No. He would never run away."

Mortimer put his arm around his daughter's shoulder to lead her from the room.

"Remember what I told you, Carlo," he warned.

Angus watched helplessly as Rosemary walked away. She hesitated for a moment and turned around. Perhaps she sensed that Angus was nearby, for her eyes desperately searched the room as her father pulled her out the door.

Angus caught a glimpse of Harriet and the Maestro, wearing his tuxedo, waiting in the narrow corridor. They looked worried.

"Is there any sign of him? We've been looking everywhere," said Harriet.

"Nothing yet," growled Mortimer. "Minnie will have to do the best she can."

Angus watched as Harriet gave Rosemary a reassuring hug. "Don't worry, sweetie. I'm sure we'll find him."

Carlo jumped up and slammed the door to his dressing room. "Fools!" he grumbled. He angrily kicked the cage with his boot, then went back to admiring himself in the mirror.

*Poor Rosemary,* Angus thought in despair. *I must get out of here. I must escape!* He began gnawing on one of the metal bars. Nothing happened, so he tried gnawing on another, and another. No matter how furiously he chewed, it was no use. His teeth were not strong enough to make even the smallest dent. He climbed to the top of the cage and pushed against the latch with all his might, but he knew that was hopeless too. There didn't seem to be any way he could escape from the cage, or from the fate that Carlo had in store for him.

# Carlo's Button

Angus hated his rusty wire prison. Even though it seemed useless, he still gnawed at the bars relentlessly, trying each one, testing to see if there might be one that was loose or almost rusted through. While he worked away on the bars, he listened. He could hear the whole performance— the orchestra, the applause, the chorus, and the fiery, emotional solos. Hearing the music softly, muted by the walls that separated him from the stage, reminded him of the rainy night in the alley so many weeks ago, when he first heard that faint, irresistible sound.

Tonight, for the first time in a long time, he didn't have to worry about frightening Minnie into hitting her high note. But he longed to be onstage, to be swept away by the sounds, colors, lights, and motion. He could feel the power and the majesty of the music from the top of his quivering ears down to the tip of his tail. Minnie's beautiful voice soared effortlessly, like a magnificent bird taking flight.

*She's wonderful*, he thought. But listening to all those familiar sounds from his miserable little cage made him feel terribly alone. And his chest hurt with a horrible aching pain he had never felt before.

The door opened and Carlo burst into his dressing room. He squirted his throat with a spray bottle and mopped his forehead. Then he peered under his dressing table, his eyes narrow and cruel.

"Are you still alive down there?" he snarled.

Angus crept into a corner of the cage. He wished he could ask for some food and a drop of water. But what was the use? Carlo didn't care.

"Why do I listen to Minnie?" Carlo muttered. "I should just throw you in the River Thames— get rid of you once and for all. Meddling little rat.

You'll see. One way or another, you'll be gone soon."

Carlo seemed to forget about Angus as he scrutinized himself in his mirror. He puffed out his chest and fussed with his costume. As he tugged at his jacket, one of the brass buttons popped off and fell on the floor with a *clink*. The button bounced, then rolled right up to Angus's cage and came to a stop. Thinking quickly, Angus reached out, pulled it into the cage, and covered it with his jacket.

Carlo cursed in Italian. He bent over and rummaged through the clutter on the floor looking for his missing button, then stopped abruptly and listened to the music.

"My cue...," he mumbled. He grabbed his rubber dagger and stuffed it in his belt. He examined himself one more time in the mirror, cursed again at the missing button, and ran out the door. He was in such a hurry, he left the door open. What a stroke of luck! Now Angus could see out into the passageway.

A few tired performers shuffled past the door, heading for their dressing rooms. Others rushed by in the oppposite direction to get to their positions on time. Angus listened carefully. The music

told him they were in Act Four, nearing the end of the opera, and he had not heard Minnie's high note. No roar of applause from the audience. Nothing. Was Mortimer going to be right? Perhaps, without Angus's help, there would be no high note for Minnie tonight.

The chatter in the corridor sounded anxious. Angus could hear bits of conversation as people passed by the doorway.

"I wouldn't want to be in her shoes . . ."

"If Mortimer tugs on his mustache one more time . . ."

"Minnie looks nervous . . ."

Giulio Gatto, the baritone, strode into his dressing room across the hall. He was followed by his girlfriend, the soprano who played Mercedes, one of Carmen's friends. Angus tried to hear what they were saying, but they were whispering too softly to each other. Their faces told the story, though; they looked worried.

A young man rushed by the door, but he came back just as quickly. He poked his head into Carlo's dressing room and looked around.

Angus jumped up. *P.J. Hendricks! What's he doing here?*

Seeing only an empty room, P.J. turned his attention to Giulio's dressing room across the hall.

"Excuse me," he said, a little out of breath.

Giulio and his lady friend looked up from their whispered conversation.

"So sorry to intrude," P.J. apologized. "Could you tell me where I might find Mortimer or Rosemary Brimley?"

"They are both backstage, I think, sir," said Giulio. "Or perhaps Miss Rosemary is onstage right now. I don't know. Everything is very confused tonight. Nothing is as it should be, I'm afraid."

P.J. scowled. "Can you fill me in? What's going on? I got a message from Mr. Brimley earlier that the little mouse is missing. But that's all I know. Have they found him yet?"

"No, no. He is gone. Vanished," said Giulio, shaking his head. "Mr. Brimley and Miss Rosemary are very upset, of course. And Miss McGraw! No one knows what is going to happen, or even if she will attempt her high note tonight."

"Thanks," said P.J. "And good luck!"

He dashed off toward the stairs that led up to the stage.

Giulio fastened his red satin cape over his black and gold toreador costume. He tossed the cape over his shoulder with a flourish, then motioned toward the door. "Shall we go see what happens, my angel?" He and his girlfriend hurried away to watch the final tragic scene.

The music was building to a frightening pitch. Angus nervously clutched the bars of his cage and listened. Don José and Carmen were in the middle of their quarrel. Soon Don José would have to "stab" Carmen, and it would be too late for Minnie to try to hit her note. Carmen was singing passionately, No, no, she would never love him! Then, finally, she tried to hit that impossible note. Her voice soared higher and higher—then suddenly stopped. A gasp rose from the audience. The orchestra kept playing, but Minnie was no longer singing. There was a long, painful pause. Angus held his breath.

He imagined the people onstage, frozen, not knowing what to do. He pictured the Maestro and the orchestra wondering whether they should continue playing—or not. Then he heard Carmen start to sing again, and he breathed a sigh of relief.

*Good for you, Minnie,* he thought. But Minnie's voice had changed. She sounded different, somehow.

A minute later she recovered and managed to play her death scene in her normal voice. Still clinging to the bars of his cage, his ears straining to hear every note, Angus imagined the final emotional scene where the "Toreador Song" echoes from within the bullfight arena, and the crowd surges out through the gates. Escamillo enters the square, proud and victorious, only to find his beloved lying there on the ground with Don José standing over her. Don José, his voice weeping, sings, "Carmen! Carmen! I adored you."

Angus heard the orchestra play the two long, dramatic chords as the curtain came down. The opera was over.

The audience applauded and there were a few shouts of "Bravo!" but it was nothing like the wild cheering when Minnie hit her incredible note and shattered the champagne glasses.

Angus listened to the curtain calls. *Oh, no!* he thought. *Did someone boo?*

In a few minutes he started to see the weary performers as they headed back to their dressing rooms. They were unusually quiet, their faces grim. Giulio Gatto returned with his lady friend to the dressing room across the hall. He tossed his cape onto a chair.

"I guess she needed the mouse, after all," he grumbled.

⁓

The door to Minnie's dressing room slammed with a bang.

"Go away! I don't want to see anyone. Leave me alone!" she cried.

Angus could hear her sob while Mortimer, outside her door, tried to console her.

"Minnie, darling," he cooed, "try to calm down. Ther-r-re's no such thing as a problem that cannot be solved. You can count on me to fix this. Just give me a little time."

"Go away!" she yelled again.

Mortimer heaved a heavy sigh. He began to pace in the corridor. Angus watched anxiously as Mortimer passed back and forth in front of Carlo's door, first one way, then the other, his brow furrowed, his head bowed in thought.

"Daddy?"

Angus jumped up and shook the bars of his cage as hard as he could. *Rosemary!* She was in the corridor, just beyond the door. If only he could see her. *Rosemary!*

"Yes, Rosie. What is it?" Her father's voice was gentle.

"I was thinking. If we find Angus, everything will be all right again, won't it? I mean, with Minnie and the tour."

"Yes, I suppose so. But I don't want you to get your hopes too high. We've looked everywhere, and . . . ," Mortimer paused, "there is a chance—horrible as it is—we might have to think about replacing him."

Angus gulped. *What?*

"No, Daddy, no! We couldn't possibly! Absolutely not!"

Angus had never heard Rosemary sound angry before. Flustered, she continued, "Anyway, Mr. Hendricks has an idea, don't you, Mr. Hendricks?"

"Yes. With your permission, sir," said P.J., "I'll write another article—this time, about the mysterious disappearance of everyone's favorite mouse. He has a lot of fans out there now, and I'm sure they would be willing to help look for him. I was thinking we could offer a reward for his safe return—no questions asked."

Angus tried to see everyone who was gathered out in the corridor, but the only one in his view was Mortimer. The dark expression on Mortimer's face brightened. "Yes. That's an excellent idea," he replied. "By all means, go ahead and write the story. If Angus is out there somewhere, maybe someone will find him."

Mortimer pulled at his mustache thoughtfully. "I have one favor to ask you, though, Hendricks."

"Of course. What can I do?"

Mortimer lowered his voice to almost a whisper. "Please don't mention anything in your article about what Rosemary did for Minnie tonight. Can that remain our little secret?"

"Absolutely," P.J. answered softly. "I don't see any reason why that has to come out. I can understand why you would want to protect Miss McGraw as much as possible."

Mortimer smiled. "Minnie would be mortified indeed. But it's not really Minnie I want to protect so much as my little Rosemary here." He put his arm around his daughter and pulled her closer.

Now Angus could see a little of her back, her long hair in a braid, and her apron tied neatly in a bow. Mortimer continued, "She proved tonight that she has a rare and wonderful gift, very much like her mother. I'm sorry I didn't recognize it until tonight. But she's still very young, and a young voice is delicate. She needs time, and patience, and training to develop her talent. I don't want people pressuring her to perform. Someday . . ."

Mortimer was too emotional to continue. A painful lump rose in Angus's throat. It had been Rosemary's beautiful voice he heard when Minnie suddenly couldn't sing. How wonderful!

She had sung Minnie's part for her—her very first time singing onstage—and her father loved it. Tears were in Mortimer's eyes as he gave Rosemary another squeeze. He looked at P.J. seriously. "I'm counting on you, Hendricks. The less people know, the better."

"You can trust me, Mr. Brimley," said P.J. "I would never do anything to harm Rosemary. But I'm afraid you'll have to excuse me if I'm going to make my deadline with that story."

"Of course. Off with you, then," said Mortimer, shaking P.J.'s hand.

P.J. extended his hand to Rosemary. At last she turned around so Angus could see her face. She took P.J.'s hand.

"Congratulations! You were brilliant tonight," he said, his voice still lowered so Minnie wouldn't hear. "And you sounded fabulous."

Rosemary blushed. "Thank you, Mr. Hendricks. And thank you for everything you're doing to help find Angus. I'm sorry I didn't trust you sooner. I hope you can forgive me."

"I'll make a deal with you. I'll forgive you if you call me P.J. from now on."

Rosemary managed a weak smile. "It's a deal."

P.J. grinned. "I'll be in touch!" Then he whirled around and dashed off.

Angus heard a clatter and commotion in the corridor as P.J. apparently almost knocked someone over with his camera bag. Then he watched as Mortimer and Rosemary turned to leave. Rosemary peered into Carlo's dressing room as she had earlier that day, her eyes searching and sad.

Angus tried to rattle the bars of his dismal cage.

"Angus?" she whispered.

"Come along, dear," said her father.

"I thought I heard something."

"You're exhausted. I'm taking you back to the hotel."

"But, Daddy . . ."

"No arguments from you, lass! You need to rest. Harriet and the Maestro will keep looking for him."

Angus squeaked as loud as he could, but it was too late. They were gone.

He slumped to the floor, his eyes moist and his whiskers quivering. They would never find him . . . never.

Mortimer's words rang in his ears. *Replace me?* he thought in horror. How could Mortimer ever consider such a horrible thing? He couldn't let that happen.

*I can't give up! Rosemary needs me.* He pulled himself together and began pacing back and forth like Mortimer so often did. *I need a plan,* he thought, more determined than ever to escape.

Beneath Angus's tweed jacket, Carlo's brass button gleamed.

# Change of Heart

Carlo stalked into his dressing room in a foul mood. He threw his cap down on the floor and tugged off his jacket. Harriet Underwood appeared in the doorway behind him.

"You sent for me, Mr. Grimaldi?"

"Yes. I've lost a button again. Here!" He tossed his jacket at Harriet. Fortunately, she caught it just before it hit her in the face.

Harriet frowned at Carlo's rude behavior. She examined the jacket. "I don't think I have any more buttons like these. You don't happen to have the one that fell off, do you?"

"Signora, I have more important things to do than look for buttons. If you sewed them on better, they would not keep falling off!"

Harriet scowled at him, insulted. "I suppose I will just have to replace them all." She put on her glasses to take a closer look. "It's these metal buttons. The sharp edges cut right through the thread. I'll replace them and have the jacket back to you in time for tomorrow night's performance."

"Ha!" he sneered. "If there *is* a performance."

"Whatever do you mean, Mr. Grimaldi?"

"Did you hear our famous soprano tonight? What a pathetic performance! How long do you think audiences will pay to hear her sing like that? I was embarrassed to be on the same stage with her."

"Mr. Grimaldi! Please keep your voice down. Miss McGraw is right next door. She'll hear you."

"Bah!" scoffed Carlo, as he sat down at his dressing table and began to wipe off his makeup. He motioned abruptly for her to leave. Lifting her chin proudly, Harriet took the jacket and left without saying another word.

"I'm surrounded by incompetent idiots,"

muttered Carlo. He smeared cold cream over his face and rubbed it around. His heavy black eyebrows disappeared and his rosy cheeks faded. He wiped it all away with a cloth, splashed cologne on his face, and combed back his dark, greasy hair.

Hidden under the dressing table, Angus huddled in the far corner of the cage and hoped that Carlo wouldn't remember he was there. Every time Carlo's big, booted foot bumped into the cage, Angus cringed. He tried to keep still so he wouldn't attract any attention; he was longing to peek under his jacket and examine the shiny metal button. He wished Carlo would leave.

A soft *tap, tap, tap* on the door made Carlo grumble in Italian under his breath.

"Come in."

The door opened and Minnie entered wearing her pink satin dressing gown. She quietly closed the door. Her eyes were red from crying.

"Are you mad at me?" she asked, her voice quavering.

Carlo sighed and went to her, put his arms around her, and spoke to her in the same soothing way that Mortimer always did. "Oh, my poor little sparrow! How could I ever be angry with you? You sang like an angel tonight, as you always do. What does it matter that you didn't hit the high note? You are, and you always will be, the greatest prima donna. People will flock to hear you whether you shatter some silly glasses or not."

Minnie blinked. "Do you really think so?"

"Of course I do. I'll tell you what: you go change into something *bellisima* and I will take you out tonight. I'm in the mood for pasta. We'll talk about it over a lovely dinner."

This idea made Minnie smile. She turned to leave, but then she stopped and pointed under the dressing table. "Is he all right?" she asked.

"The rat? He's alive—unfortunately."

❧

Carlo switched off the light and closed the door. At last, Angus was alone. The button! He couldn't wait to look at it. He waited for his eyes to adjust to the darkened room. Minnie and Carlo must have been among the last people to leave. The opera house was unusually quiet. Angus would have the whole night to try to escape, if only the button could be of some use. He was about to move when he heard an unexpected sound outside. Footsteps were coming back down the corridor.

"Carlo!" It was Minnie's voice. "Go ahead and hail a taxi. I forgot something. I'll be out in a moment."

Angus heard a rustling noise, then the door opened and the light went on. Minnie rushed over to the dressing table, pushed away some of the clutter and knelt down. She looked beautiful in a bright red dress and diamond earrings that glittered. She carefully held up a gloved hand to shield her eyes, and tried her best to avoid looking at him.

"Oh, dreadful little mouse—*please* don't move! If you move, I might scream," she said, her voice trembling. "I don't know why I'm doing this." Then she opened her evening bag and took something out. Angus cowered further into the corner as she reached over to drop something into the cage.

*Poison!* Terrified, he covered his nose with his paws.

Instead, a handful of nuts, raisins, and bits of sweet, buttery shortbread rained down on him. Then Minnie took one of her fancy embroidered handkerchiefs, soaked it with Carlo's expensive bottled water, and pushed it through the bars.

"I'm sorry . . . it's the best I could do," she said. She moved one finger away from her eyes for a fraction of a second and gingerly peeked at him. Angus wanted to thank her, but he was so

surprised he couldn't move. He couldn't even squeak. Minnie got up and hurried to the door. Before she turned out the light, she hesitated; Angus thought he saw her shudder.

"Good night," she whispered. Then she was gone.

∽

Angus was weak from hunger. He couldn't remember the last time he had eaten. Quickly he stuffed his mouth with food and chewed furiously, completely forgetting his table manners. Rosemary would be shocked if she could see him now. But she would be even more horrified if she saw how dreadfully he had been treated.

He thought of Minnie as he gobbled down a delicious, meaty cashew. She didn't hate him, after all. Truthfully, she was probably too scared of him to like him very much, but at least she didn't want him to starve to death in the horrid little cage. She had a good heart. But Carlo was different—he was dangerous. All Carlo cared about was—Carlo.

Angus sucked some water from Minnie's handkerchief. Thankful for her kindness, he started to feel much better and stronger. He nibbled on some shortbread, then washed his whiskers quickly with his paws. He couldn't wait any longer. He crept out of the corner toward the button. He lifted up his jacket and looked at it. Even in the darkness it had a magical gleam.

He examined it carefully. It was just a cheap, hollow, costume button, but the sight of it made Angus's heart leap. The top was decorated with a crude military design, and a thin metal lip was bent around the bottom. Yes! Some of the edges were sharp, just as Harriet had said. Perhaps if he could bend the metal and straighten it, he might be able to saw through one of the bars. He bit down on it with his teeth and felt it bend slightly. He bit down again and it bent a little more.

Maybe he could flatten it out just enough.

Maybe it would be sharp enough.

Maybe . . .

Angus set to work chewing on the edges of the button.

# An Argument

Noises in the corridor woke him up.

Angus rubbed his eyes and yawned. He must have fallen asleep again. He looked at the button resting in his lap. What a beautiful sight! After hours and hours of exhausting work, he had managed to flatten a section of the metal into something that vaguely resembled a saw, and judging by the tender, raw corners of his mouth, it was quite sharp indeed.

Dim light filtered into the room through its tiny window. He had been so busy, he had lost all sense of time. What day was it? Was it early morning or late afternoon? It didn't really matter—Carlo could come back at any moment and decide to get rid of him once and for all. The sooner he could escape, the sooner he could find Rosemary.

He picked up his button-saw and set to work on the rustiest of the bars.

*Scree—scree—screeeech!*

*Oh, no!* The metal saw on the metal bars made a horrible noise. He would have to work fast to finish the job before anyone came into the room. Angus sawed away furiously until his muscles ached. He sawed and sawed and sawed. A tiny dent began to appear in the bar.

After an hour or more of hard work, he had to stop and rest. He sucked on Minnie's wet handkerchief again and ate a few more nuts and raisins. While he waited for his energy to return, he listened to the unusual sounds coming from outside the room. The opera house was always bustling at night, but it was curious for there to be so much activity during the day. Strange and unfamiliar voices went up and down the corridor.

*What are they doing out there?* he wondered.

Suddenly he had a frightening thought. What if

the tour had been canceled? If Minnie couldn't hit her high note, maybe the opera company was being sent home. Or perhaps Carlo had talked Minnie into quitting. Maybe they were packing up everything to return to New York. Certainly Carlo would dispose of him now—or leave him alone in London to starve in his cage. He had to get out. He had to get out and find Rosemary before it was too late!

Angus shuddered at the thought of being left behind. He would never see Rosemary again, or Mortimer, or Harriet, or the Maestro. He would never again sleep on his canopy bed or curled up in Rosemary's pocket. He wouldn't sip tea with her in the afternoon, or share her muffins and jam. And what of the music he loved? If he somehow managed to survive, he would still be in the opera house—but he would be miserable and alone. How could the music sound as beautiful when his heart was broken?

Angus smoothed his whiskers, took a deep breath, and set to work again. The dent in the rusty bar was getting deeper.

Angus's paws were sore and bloody. He was exhausted, but he set down his button-saw, jumped up, and danced a little jig. He twirled around and around until he fell over, dizzy with joy. He had done it. He had sawed through the bar. He was free!

He gathered up his precious tweed jacket. Even though it was stained and smelly, it was his only possession, and it reminded him of happier days. He hoped that Harriet could have it cleaned for him—if he ever saw her again.

Angus pushed on the bar. He pushed again with all his might. How could a rusty old bar be so strong? Why wouldn't it bend? He gritted his teeth and pushed, and groaned, and pushed some more. It barely budged.

Just then, the door to the room flew open, and Minnie and Carlo came in. They closed the door behind them. Carlo flopped down in his chair, leaving Minnie standing.

"Oh, I find this very amusing," he said with a smirk. "Everyone is going to so much trouble to find that ugly little rodent, and he's right here under their noses the whole time."

He gave the cage a kick, and laughed heartily

as he ran his fingers through his thick, dark hair. He lowered his voice to a harsh whisper. "Minnie, I overheard a crazy rumor today. I heard Mortimer is secretly auditioning little rats to take his place—but they are such vile, stupid creatures they never do what they are told. Some of them even bite!"

Minnie looked horrified. "Bite?" she gasped.

Carlo continued his tirade. "The whole thing is outrageous! Mortimer Brimley has turned the opera into a circus. There must be people all over the city running around trying to catch the rat and collect the reward. Did you see all the people lined up outside with their little rat cages?"

"And Mortimer and Rosemary are upstairs in the office interviewing every one of them," offered Minnie. "I do feel badly for little Rosemary, though. She seems so sad."

"Bah!" said Carlo. "She'll get over it. I think it's time we dispose of the vermin."

"Oh, no!" cried Minnie. "We can't do that! I could never have that on my conscience. Besides, I think I have a much better idea."

"Hmmph! I'm going to get rid of him and be done with it." Carlo reached for the cage.

"No, listen to me, Carlo. This is our chance to steal the spotlight back from the little mouse. We will 'find' him ourselves! We'll return him to Mortimer and Rosemary, and then we can *refuse* the reward. Don't you see? It's perfect. That reporter— what's his name? Henshaw? He'll write a wonderful story about us in his newspaper, and we'll be the heroes who found the mouse. People will love us more than ever!"

Carlo's eyes gleamed for a moment, but he was skeptical. "And then what, Minnie? Will you go back to being terrified before every performance? All my planning, all my effort, and the trouble I went to to help you will be for nothing."

Minnie turned red. "All the trouble *you* went to? We did it together, remember? For both of us. And besides, your plan didn't work, did it? You said I didn't need the mouse. You said everything would be fine. But everything isn't fine. It's an absolute disaster! If I don't hit my high note tonight, we could all be packing up and going home tomorrow!"

"Yes, yes, it is a disaster!" Carlo shouted. "And whose fault is that? Why can't you hit that high note, miss fancy pants *stupida* prima donna?"

Now Minnie turned purple. "W-w-what?" she

sputtered. "How dare you insult me? How dare you blame me? I thought you loved me! Mortimer was right about you. Well, fine!" she exclaimed, her voice quavering and her eyes flashing. "This is just fine!"

Minnie became fearless in her rage. She pushed her way past Carlo, bent down, and grabbed the cage from under the dressing table.

"I'm taking this cage up to the office and telling Mortimer everything. I'm telling him it was all your idea, and you forced me to help you! Now we'll see who is *stupido!*"

Minnie stormed toward the door.

"Wait!" cried Carlo.

"It's too late for apologies, Carlo."

"No, wait," he pleaded. "Look at the cage."

They both stared.

The rusty cage was empty.

# 14

# Brutus

"He can't have gone far," cried Carlo, his black eyes narrowing. "I'll find him if I have to tear this place apart. He'll be sorry he ever crossed paths with Carlo Grimaldi!"

He began lifting rumpled clothes from the floor and wildly tossing them everywhere. Socks, shoes, and boots flew through the air as he searched frantically for the missing mouse.

Minnie realized that Angus could be anywhere, including crawling up her dress, so she climbed on top of the chair. One of Carlo's slippers sailed past her nose.

"Carlo! Don't be ridiculous! He's gone. You'll never find him."

Carlo looked up from the floor, his face red. He smoothed his tousled hair and smiled sweetly. "I'm sure you are right, my pet. Anyway, soon they will give up their search and our lives will go back to normal. The rat will be forgotten and the spotlight will be on us again—as it should be."

Carlo got up and held out a hand to help Minnie down from the chair. He forced a laugh. "I'm sorry I was cross with you. Will you forgive your hot-blooded Italian tenor?"

Angus couldn't bear to watch anymore. He had forced the bar of the cage just enough so he could squeeze through, and now he was hiding in a narrow space behind the radiator. It was time to escape from this awful place. He stuffed his jacket under his arm and slipped through a small hole in the floor where an old steam pipe came up from the cellar. He crawled down the pipe, tail first, his toenails making little screeching sounds on the bare metal.

He thought if he could get down to the cellar, then he might find some way to climb back up into the opera house. He had no idea where he might come out, and he really didn't care—just as long as it wasn't Carlo's dressing room. Somehow, he needed to get upstairs. He had overheard Minnie say that Mortimer and Rosemary were in the office. He must get up to that office!

Freedom was so exhilarating that Angus became reckless; he should have been more careful. He started to slide down the pipe out of control, faster and faster, until he hit a slippery patch. He lost his grip and fell with a *plop* onto the cold cellar floor.

Angus got up and brushed himself off. The cellar was dark and cavernous. It reminded him of that first night in the old Brooklyn Opera House, when he had followed the sound of the music into the cellar and then up onto the stage. That was the fateful night that began his opera career—when Minnie shattered the chandelier. Now, here he was, back in a dreary cellar, filthy and miserable once more. Tired and sore as he was, he knew he had to keep moving if he was ever going to find Rosemary.

*There's no time to lose,* he thought. He began to scurry toward the rumbling roar of the enormous furnace that heated the opera house. Maybe he could find an easy way out of the cellar and back up to Mortimer's office. A rope—a post—anything.

*Clang!* A shovel crashed down just a hair from the tip of Angus's tail. Angus leaped into the air in terror. A great, hulking, sweaty man was swinging the shovel toward him again.

*Clang!* Angus leaped in the opposite direction.

"Brutus! Where are ya? I got one for ya! He's a mite scrawny, but he's a lively one."

Angus was running now, darting this way and that way, not knowing where to go. Frantic, he looked for the nearest small hole to escape into. Too late! An ornery-looking black cat, with scars on his ears and one eye missing, pounced silently onto the cellar floor in front of him. They froze, looking at each other for a long moment. The cat's tail twitched menacingly.

"Get him, Brutus!" cried the man, with a laugh.

Angus took his beloved tweed jacket and threw it in the cat's face. Brutus yowled and ripped the little jacket into shreds with his claws, but Angus had the instant he needed to escape. He ran faster than he had ever run in his life. He could hear the cat's paws hitting the cellar floor behind him with each step. He could feel the cat's hot breath on his ears. Once or twice the cat stepped on the tip of Angus's tail and he almost stumbled, but it made him run even faster. Where was a hole?

Angus flew around a corner and straight into the narrow neck of an old bottle. Brutus leaped on top of him, hissing angrily. Angus clutched his heaving chest, but he was safe inside the bottle.

Back near the furnace, the big workman

chuckled to himself. "Ha, ha! One less mouse in the opera house. Good ol' Brutus will crush his bones, for sure!"

Angus heard what the man said and cowered in the bottle as Brutus's fishy breath steamed up the glass.

# A Magic Suit

The stale air in the bottle was foul, but Angus forced himself to take slow, deep breaths. It felt like his thundering heart was going to explode. He needed to calm down and think. He rubbed a small spot on the glass with his paw until it was clean enough for him to peek out into the dingy cellar. A few bare lightbulbs hanging from the ceiling cast a dull, yellow light, and created eerie and confusing shadows. It was hard to tell what was real and what was shadow. Angus squinted through the glass, searching for some means of escape.

What was it Mortimer always said? "There is no such thing as a problem that cannot be solved."

*I need a plan,* he thought.

Brutus crouched in front of Angus, his golden eye staring at him, narrow and cruel. He grew impatient and swatted the bottle with his paw. It spun around several times, then skittered across the cellar floor. Brutus enjoyed this game, so he batted at the bottle again and again. The bottle spun and rolled, spun and rolled, as Brutus joyfully leaped in the air, chased after it, and swatted it tirelessly. Angus tumbled around inside, getting bruised and dizzy. After several minutes of this torture, the bottle clattered dangerously close to the furnace and came to rest just a few inches from the big man's shoe. He was sitting on a small wooden stool under one of the lightbulbs. Brutus sauntered into the dim light, panting.

"Hey! What's all this racket?" grumbled the man. "Brutus, can't you see I'm trying to read this here newspaper?"

The papers rustled as he turned the page. A minute later he cried out, "Criminy! It says here they're looking for some mouse that's gone missing.

And I might have had me a reward too. Well, too late now, eh, Brutus? You just had yourself an expensive dinner—if that was indeed the famous mouse you just ate up!"

The man threw the paper down, grabbed the cat, and pulled him into his lap. The bottle was so grimy he didn't see the mouse cringing inside. Angus thought for a moment that he could try to get the man's attention, but it was too risky. Brutus would pounce on him in a flash. The man coughed and gave the bottle a good, hard kick that sent it careening off into the shadows. Brutus tried to leap after it, but the man held him fast.

"Now, now," he said, "be a good kitty and sit here with me awhile." He rubbed the cat's ears and Brutus started to purr. "It's a shame about that lady singer. She's a pretty one, and nice too. She smiled at me, ya know. Yeah. She was in a big hurry going somewhere all dressed up fancy-like and sparkly, but she looked right at me and smiled." He breathed a heavy sigh. "Poor lady. No doubt they'll all be packing up if she don't hit that note again soon."

With his deep, gravelly voice, the big man began to hum a hodgepodge of melodies from *Carmen*.

Twenty feet away, Angus tried to clear his head. He was dazed from his wild ride in the bottle. Then he noticed something that made his situation even more desperate—a long crack curled around the bottle like a snake. One more kick or knock on the hard cellar floor and the glass might break. Panic seized him and he felt hot tears well up in his eyes. What a horrible predicament he was in. If he couldn't get out of the cellar, he might never see Rosemary again. But he had not come this far to fail now. Angrily he brushed the tears away with his paws. He took a moment to smooth his whiskers and quickly wash his ears and tail. He could always think better when he felt tidy. He dared to poke his head out of the bottle and have a look around.

What was that? The darkness and shadows made it difficult to see. It appeared that the floor above was supported by huge cement pillars, but here and there a few of the old wooden posts were still in place. Angus could easily climb up a wooden post, if he could get to it. The ceiling was covered with a maze of beams, pipes, wires, and air ducts. All he had to do was get to safety at the top of the post, then scamper along the old pipes until he found a way back into the opera house. It sounded easy. Unfortunately, with his sharp claws, Brutus could climb up a wooden post too. What Angus needed was a good head start.

He looked over at the big workman and Brutus curled up on his lap. They looked peaceful. The black cat was still purring as the man stroked him and softly hummed the "Toreador Song." Nevertheless, Angus was quite certain Brutus was watching him with his golden eye.

He crept back into the bottle and took a few small steps on the rounded surface of the glass. The bottle rolled quietly for two inches. He peeked out again. Brutus had not flinched. Inside the bottle, Angus took a few more small steps, and the bottle rolled three more inches. Little by little the bottle silently inched its way toward the wooden post.

Angus had no idea how long it took him to roll the bottle close to the post. It might have been an hour or more. Finally, he peeked again to look at the man and Brutus. They seemed to be sleeping. He looked at the post and judged the distance—only two feet away at the most! Carefully, he crept out of the mouth of the bottle. He filled his lungs with fresh air, ready to make his dash, and cast one final glance at the man and Brutus.

He squeaked in horror! The man was snoring with his greasy chin resting on his chest, but Brutus was gone! He thought of running back to the safety of the bottle. But in the next instant he was seized by a fierce, blinding rage at the evil cat who stood in the way of all his efforts to escape.

*No!* he thought. *I won't let him stop me. I can make it!*

Perhaps it was craziness, or perhaps it was courage—without even looking for where Brutus might be lurking, Angus bounded toward the post, his feet barely touching the ground. His tiny toenails grabbed onto the rough wood and he dashed up the post, round and round like a corkscrew, faster and faster. Out of the shadows appeared a dark phantom—a dreadful black demon, hissing and spitting foul venom. Brutus lunged at the post, his claws ripping into the wood, sending dust and splinters into the air. But Brutus's strength and speed were no match for

Angus's determination. Hearing Brutus scrambling up the post just inches behind him only made Angus go faster. He climbed all the way to the ceiling and jumped onto a narrow pipe that stretched on and on into the dark recesses of the cellar. Angus ran and ran, his feet pinging on the cool metal.

Brutus, clinging to the post, yowled angrily.

"Criminy!" shouted the man. "Quiet down, Brutus! I was having a lovely dream about me and the pretty lady. Ah! Now you've ruined it!"

Angus was never so anxious to be far, far away from a place in his life. He never wanted to see a dismal, dark cellar again, or the big hulking man, or the hideous one-eyed cat. But he remembered the slippery patch that made him fall into the cellar in the first place, and decided to slow down and be more careful. He began to search for a hole in the floor above him. He was so hungry and thin, even a small crack would be big enough for him to crawl through. He scampered back and forth along the maze of pipes that crisscrossed the ceiling. Finally, a speck of light caught his eye. When he got closer he could see that it came from a small crack in the flooring where a pipe went up into the opera house above. A dreadful thought occurred to him: it might be the same hole he had used to escape from Carlo's dressing room.

*What if I end up back in the same awful place I started?* he moaned.

He poked his head up into the narrow space and squeezed through. He stood in a small room, hidden behind a radiator. He rubbed his eyes and blinked in the bright light. Cautiously, he peeped out. He couldn't believe his luck. He knew this room! He had been there many times with Rosemary. His heart flooded with relief and joy—he was in Harriet Underwood's wardrobe room! There, against the wall, were the racks of costumes that needed her attention. There, in the corner, was the trunk where the Maestro sat while she measured Angus for his new clothes. And there, on the floor by her chair, was her sewing basket, brimming with spools of thread, pincushions, ribbons, and swatches of lace and fabric. How fondly he remembered the day when she surprised him by giving him his beautiful tweed

jacket, now torn to shreds, and the wonderful tuxedo he had never worn.

Near the sewing basket, Angus saw a pile of
pastel silks on the floor that looked like a soft,
comfortable cloud. A wave of exhaustion swept
over him, and for a moment, he considered curl-
ing up on such a lovely, soft bed.

The billowy mountain of silk tempted him until
he caught a glimpse of his feet. Then he looked in
disgust at his paws and fur. He was filthy from the
top of his ears to the tip of his tail—covered in
dust balls, cobwebs, and grime from the cellar.
How could he make his reappearance looking like
such a frightful mess? Rosemary wouldn't recognize him.

He scurried back to where he had seen a small
puddle of water that had leaked out of the radiator. Angus liked to be clean, but he was never
fond of water. Nevertheless, for Rosemary's sake,
he splashed in the puddle and scrubbed himself
furiously, paying special attention to his feet, his
whiskers, and his tail. When he was finished, he
was definitely more presentable, but he was still
exhausted. Every bone and muscle in his body
ached from his ordeal.

*Perhaps if I wait here, Harriet will come back…*
He was considering this new possibility with a glimmer of hope when his ears suddenly pricked up at a familiar sound.

At any other time, that sound would have delighted him as it echoed through the opera house. The sweet jumble of instruments tuning up for the night's performance was a peculiarly exciting sort of music. But now it sounded more like a jangling alarm clock, waking him up, telling him that time was running out. It must be later than he thought. In a few minutes the curtain would be going up. There was no time to get up to the office. No time to look for Rosemary. Certainly no time to rest!

Angus knew what he had to do. Somehow, he had to get to the stage. He remembered what he overheard Minnie say: they could all be packing up tomorrow if she didn't hit her high note.

Minnie had been kind to him despite her fear of mice. Now he needed to help her hit that high note one more time. Tonight, the whole opera company needed him. Rosemary and Mortimer needed him. He couldn't let them all down.

Angus made a dash for the door. It was

shut tight, but he was sure he could squeeze under it and get into the corridor. He sighed and tried to ignore his exhaustion as he passed by the lovely cloud of silk. He had to get to the stage. He had to scare Minnie—then he and Rosemary could be together again. He scurried across the wardrobe room, then—he stopped. He turned around and looked back at Harriet's sewing basket. Something had caught his eye. Something wonderful and irresistible. His tuxedo! He ran back, climbed up into the basket, and slipped on the jacket.

He had no time to examine himself in the mirror, but instantly he felt better. He ran his paws gently over the fine, smooth material. It was like a magic suit. He felt bigger, stronger. He felt invincible. He took a deep breath and ran for the door.

# 16

# Never Give Up

Angus thought he knew his way around the back-stage corridors of the opera house, but he had always been riding high up in Rosemary's hand or in her pocket. Everything appeared entirely different from far down below on the floor. All the doors to the dressing rooms looked exactly the same, and the long, narrow corridor seemed to stretch on forever. Adding to his discomfort were all the people hurrying back and forth; every-one was in their last-minute rush to get to their places before the curtain went up.

He did not want to be trampled, but he did not

want to be noticed either. Not now. Not after all the perils he had already endured. There was just a handful of people he knew he could trust— Rosemary and Mortimer, and Harriet and the Maestro. With a little luck he might find one of them and get their attention. Everyone else frightened him; they were not his friends, and he feared they might even hand him over to his greatest enemy—the fiendish Carlo Grimaldi. He couldn't let that happen.

He waited for his chance, then scampered down the corridor and ducked into a doorway to catch his breath. His heart raced a little faster when he heard the audience applauding, and the first thrilling notes of the overture. The opera was beginning. He waited until the coast was clear again, then ran a little further and ducked into the next doorway. More people hurried by, so he shrank into the shadows.

A door opened across the hall. Light spilled out into the corridor, and Giulio Gatto stood in the doorway. He didn't make his first appearance until Act Two, so he was still wearing his blue brocade dressing gown. He stood in the doorway as if he were leaving, but he lingered there, smiling.

"*Cara mia*," he said softly, "when I sing tonight, I sing only for you."

A soft, feminine laugh came from inside the dressing room.

Giulio continued, "I have a terrible confession— I hope that Miss McGraw fails to shatter the champagne glasses tonight. Can you guess why?"

"Why don't you tell me?" the woman's voice teased.

"Because I want to take you to Paris. Just you and I, alone, with no prying eyes watching us. If the tour ends, we could be there tomorrow!"

Angus groaned when he remembered that Giulio was infatuated with the soprano who played Mercedes, Carmen's friend. If Giulio continued to stand there and talk, Angus would be trapped, unable to move.

"Can you imagine us together in the City of Lights, my angel?"

Angus squirmed. Giulio's flirting might go on and on. Angus thought of making a dash for the next doorway, but Giulio kept looking around, checking the corridor for people who might come along and disturb their privacy. Giulio might see him if he made a move.

*What a nightmare!* Angus moaned. All he could do was wait.

Angus listened to the music as it echoed down the corridor. The overture built to a crescendo and ended with a thrilling dramatic chord. Act One began. Angus could picture the curtain rising, revealing the colorful town square in Seville, bustling with soldiers and townspeople. A few minutes later, he heard the trumpet fanfare announcing the changing of the guard, and the children's chorus singing along merrily as they imitated the soldiers' march. His heart ached as he wondered if Rosemary was onstage tonight . . . waiting for him . . . hoping he might appear.

Suddenly, the woman's voice cried out in alarm from the dressing room, "Oh, good heavens! See what you do to me? I've missed my cue!" She rushed by Giulio, lightly brushing his hand as she passed. Her petticoats rustled and her brown curls bounced on her bare shoulders as she ran down the corridor and disappeared around the corner. Giulio watched her go and sighed.

Angus sighed too.

*At last!* Maybe now he could get to the stage. He watched Giulio wander down the hall to his dressing room and close the door. Angus looked up and down the corridor; the coast was clear. He skittered along as fast as he could to the next doorway and stopped. He heard voices coming, so he pressed himself into the corner and waited until they passed by. As he huddled there in the shadows, he could feel the blood pounding in his ears.

Suddenly, he felt ill. He covered his nose with his paws. *That disgusting smell!*

The scent of Carlo's cologne overwhelmed his sensitive nose and made him gag. Instantly, it brought back all the horrible memories of his imprisonment in the rusty cage. Angus peered under the door. He recognized the messy clutter of clothes and shoes strewn over the floor. He was standing in the doorway of Carlo's dressing room! Even though he knew Carlo was onstage during Act One, the sick feeling in his stomach told him he had to get away from there. Now! He rubbed the satin lapels of his tuxedo for luck. No one was coming, so he made a wild dash; he didn't stop running until he got to the end of the corridor.

His heart was racing, but he was out of danger

for the moment. A large, red fire extinguisher sitting in the corner gave him a safe place to hide.

Angus tried to catch his breath as he surveyed the situation. Amazed and relieved that he had successfully navigated to the end of the long hallway, he was now faced with another obstacle— the stairs that led to the stage. Any other time, he could have scampered up those stairs without a problem. One, two, three, and he would be at the top. But he was so weak, bruised, and exhausted that the stairs looked like a mountain towering before him. Still, he had to try. He darted up to the first step and leaped. He missed the top of the step by two inches, and landed in a heap back on the floor. Again he ran and jumped, and again he fell back down. It was no use. He was too tired, too weak. He had spent the last of his energy escaping from Brutus in the cellar. He scurried back behind the fire extinguisher and slumped into the corner, his chest heaving and his spirits sinking.

*Rosemary . . . Rosemary . . .* Even the sound of her name was comforting. As he huddled there alone and miserable, he imagined her smiling at him; he missed her soft voice, and her eyes that twinkled when she laughed. She had always been so kind, and her touch so gentle; he had trusted her from the very beginning. She was the only friend he had ever had, and he would trade all the cheese in the world to be safely curled up in her pocket.

*She's still looking for me. I know she is. If only she would come along right now and find me! If only . . .*

Angus shook himself. Wishful thinking was useless. If Mortimer had taught him nothing else, it was to take action, and never give up. He had already accomplished what was nearly impossible—he had escaped from Carlo and the awful cage, from the big hulking man, from the bottle and the cellar, and from Brutus the demon cat. Why should he be discouraged now?

*I must get up those stairs,* he told himself. He carefully brushed some dust from his tuxedo. *I'm all dressed up. I'm ready. I'll find a way.*

◦~◦

Act One came to an end with a flourish from the orchestra, and dozens of breathless performers came thundering down the stairs, all rushing to their dressing rooms to change costumes or touch up their makeup. Angus watched all the familiar people whisk past him. He shuddered when Carlo Grimaldi hurried by, wearing his corporal's uniform, his sword rattling at his side. He was followed by Minnie, but they were not speaking to each other. Minnie looked strained and nervous.

Angus's heart skipped a beat when he saw P.J. Hendricks bound down the stairs. He thought for an instant of getting his attention somehow, but P.J. hurried past him and disappeared down the corridor before Angus could make a move. Still, seeing P.J. gave him hope. Angus liked him. His instinct told him P.J. had a good heart, and given the opportunity, P.J. would not betray him.

P.J. had his cumbersome camera bag slung over his shoulder; most likely he was working on his next story for the newspaper. After all, it was a "make it or break it" night for the opera company, so there was sure to be a big story. Either they would be packing up and going home in the morning, or Minnie would miraculously hit her high note once more. Angus guessed P.J. was going to ask a few questions of the performers about the big night, and then come back to rejoin everyone standing anxiously in the wings. If P.J. came back,

Angus would be ready for him. He was starting to get an idea.

*It just might work,* he thought.

Angus peered out from behind the fire extinguisher. He was still hoping to see Rosemary or Mortimer, but they didn't come. Disappointed, he heaved a sigh. They must have stayed in the wings during the short break between Act One and Act Two. Even Harriet, who was usually bustling about everywhere, was nowhere to be seen.

A moment later the audience began to applaud politely, the performers started to hurry back to the stage, and the bassoons and strings played the first haunting notes of the prelude to Act Two. Minnie rushed by and up the stairs, wearing a colorful peasant dress, a black fringed shawl, and a red rose in her hair. Angus fidgeted. How he longed to be watching from the wings with Rosemary; Act Two of *Carmen* was their favorite.

Carmen is onstage for the entire act and sings some of the most beautiful melodies in the whole opera. It begins with a fiery Spanish dance: Carmen sings the dazzling "Gypsy Song" as the dancers whirl around her, clapping, jangling their tambourines, and stomping their heels to the Spanish rhythms. Suddenly Escamillo, the swaggering hero, enters with a crowd of admirers. He sings the famous "Toreador Song," describing the danger and the thrill of the bullfight. Finally, Don José arrives, and Carmen convinces him to run away from the army and join her and her friends in their mountain hideout. At the end of the act, everyone sings a stirring song celebrating their freedom.

Mortimer never liked to interrupt Act Two. It was too exciting and beautiful. He always tried to wait until at least Act Three to give Angus the signal. It was even better to let the suspense build and wait until Act Four.

Angus felt his heart pounding as he listened to the exciting rhythm of the "Gypsy Song" getting wilder and faster. The music, the opera—this was his world. This was where he belonged.

Minnie's powerful voice soared above the orchestra, and he could feel the thundering of the dancers' feet on the stage above him.

*Act Two is just beginning,* he thought. *I still have time.*

# Great Caesar's Ghost!

Angus closed his eyes and let the sound of the glorious music revive him. He opened his eyes again when Giulio Gatto finally came out of his dressing room, ready for his famous solo. Giulio passed by some of the Spanish dancers as they returned from the stage, breathing hard from their rollicking dance. Angus kept his eyes on the long hallway. Somewhere down there, P.J. Hendricks was finishing up his interviews. Angus was sure of it. He just had to wait for his opportunity.

A few minutes later, Giulio's rich baritone voice began to bellow the first notes of the "Toreador

Song," and as if on cue, when he sang, "Ready! On guard!" a door opened down the hall and P.J. Hendricks appeared. As P.J. started down the hall toward the stairs, Angus prepared to make his move. As soon as P.J. walked past the fire extinguisher, Angus darted out behind him and leaped onto his trouser leg.

*Thank goodness for fine English tweed!* he thought as his toenails grabbed onto the coarse woolen material. Angus had to cling tightly as P.J. bounded up the stairs; he swung wildly back and forth with every step P.J. took. But he had done it! He was up the stairs at last, and P.J. was carrying him right to the stage. He would be able to see everything and everyone who was onstage, as well as anyone who was waiting in the wings.

*P.J. might take me straight to Rosemary!* he thought happily.

P.J. stopped and stood near one of the heavy black curtains that separated the stage from the wings. Angus was dizzy with excitement. It seemed like an eternity since he had been this close to the stage. The music was almost deafening, the lights were hot, and the stage was a sea of color and motion. Angus scampered a little higher on P.J.'s trousers and took it all in. Escamillo was strutting around, describing the wild rush of the bull and the bravery of the toreador. The admiring crowd hovered around their hero.

*Where is she? Where is she?* Angus wondered, as his sharp eyes scanned every corner of the stage for a glimpse of Rosemary. He climbed higher onto P.J.'s camera bag, then up the leather strap. Too many people still obstructed his view.

Then he thought, *Oh, why not?*

He climbed onto P.J.'s shoulder. Now he could see perfectly, but still, he couldn't find Rosemary among the colorful throng of performers.

Feeling desperate, Angus decided to take a risk and get P.J.'s attention. He waited for a moment when the music was softer, then leaned up to P.J.'s ear and squeaked. The first time P.J. didn't hear him, so he squeaked again a little louder. This time P.J. turned his head and saw Angus standing on his shoulder.

"Great Caesar's ghost!" he exclaimed, then clapped his hand over his mouth for being too loud. "Angus MacMouse! Is that you?" he whispered.

Angus nodded.

"Blimey! I—I don't believe it!" he stuttered. "It's miraculous! You're alive!"

P.J. put his hand up to his shoulder so Angus could climb into his palm, then he held Angus up to his face where he could get a good look at him. He broke into a silly, boyish grin.

"It *is* you, isn't it? And looking very fine in that suit, I might add!"

They both started to giggle as relief and joy swept over them. P.J. gently tickled Angus's ears, and grinned again.

"What a brilliant little fellow you are!" he said, trying to be quiet. "I mean, here you are, after all this time! I—I'm speechless! But what am I thinking? We don't have much time! Have you seen Rosemary yet? Does she know you're here?"

Angus shook his head.

"No? Well, we had better remedy that straightaway. Hmmm . . . let's see. Where might she be?"

As they both looked toward the stage, searching for the golden hair of Rosemary Brimley, a meaty fist shot out from behind them and yanked Angus out of P.J.'s hand.

"Aha! I've got the little vermin!" rasped Carlo Grimaldi.

Angus felt the air being squeezed out of his lungs by Carlo's powerful grip. He struggled, but his arms were pinned. He squeaked pitifully.

"Excuse me, Signor Grimaldi!" exclaimed P.J. indignantly. "What do you think you're doing?"

"He's mine! I'm claiming the reward. I caught him earlier, but he escaped."

"Oh, no, you don't! You're not taking him," said P.J., grabbing Carlo's arm.

"*Si, si!* I've got him! He's mine! Let me go!" Carlo's face was crimson.

P.J. and Carlo tugged back and forth on the hand that held Angus.

"Watch out, you villain! You're hurting him!" cried P.J., no longer trying to keep his voice down.

Angus felt his ribs being crushed. He couldn't breathe. Everything was getting dim and fuzzy. Then, through the fog, he saw something large and dark hurtling toward him—P.J.'s camera bag! He heard a dull thud, and suddenly he was free. Not only was he free, he was soaring.

*I'm light as a feather,* he thought, as he sailed

162

through the air. The last thing he saw was Rosemary's face as she ran toward him. Her expression was rather odd, he thought. She looked
happy—and frightened. *Rosemary!* Then everything turned a soft, velvety black.

❦

Angus was having such a deliciously restful sleep.
He squirmed and wrinkled his nose. Why was
someone trying to disturb him? How annoying!

"Angus? Angus?" prodded a gentle voice.
"Angus?"

Grudgingly he opened one eye. A sea of blurry
faces looked down on him. He wiggled and closed
his eye again. He was so very comfortable and
sleepy.

*Go away!* he thought. *Leave me alone. Let me
sleep.*

"Angus, my brave little mouse...it's Rosemary. Please, *please* wake up."

*Rosemary?* Angus began to remember. He
remembered climbing onto P.J.'s shoulder and
then the scuffle with Carlo Grimaldi. He remembered the heavy camera bag swinging toward
him—and toward Carlo's head! He remembered

seeing Rosemary running to him. Slowly, he opened his eyes again.

P.J. Hendricks, Mortimer Brimley, Harriet Underwood, and Rosemary were looking down at him.

"I think he's coming around," said Mortimer in a hushed voice.

"Shouldn't we get a doctor?" asked P.J., looking concerned. "I mean, he's had quite a tumble."

"The doctor is coming," whispered Mortimer.

"I can't believe he's wearing his tuxedo!" sobbed Harriet, dabbing at her eyes with a handkerchief. "What a remarkable little fellow."

"Angus, are you hurt?" said Rosemary. Large, round tears were rolling down her cheeks like raindrops. "You must tell me if you're hurt."

Carefully, Angus sat up and looked around. Beyond the people hovering over him, he recognized the familiar clutter of Mortimer's makeshift office. He was sitting on the green blotter on Mortimer's desk—the very same spot he had been resting several days ago when Carlo so cruelly mousenapped him.

"Water!" said P.J., suddenly. "I'll get him some water."

Harriet always carried her thimble with her. She took it from her pocket and handed it to P.J. "Here, use this," she said, still sniffling.

P.J. returned in a few seconds with the thimble of water. "Here you go, Angus. I'm truly sorry. I was aiming for Carlo. I never meant for you to go flying like that. Really, I feel just awful."

Angus took a long, refreshing drink. He blinked, and looked at all the faces surrounding him. Not one of them wanted to hurt him, or capture him, or pounce on him, or eat him. These were all the faces of his friends. He was safe at last. His whiskers trembled with happiness and relief. He looked at Rosemary and managed a weak smile.

"Angus," she sighed, and started to reach for him, but her father stopped her hand.

"We shouldn't touch him until we know if he's all right," said Mortimer.

At that moment someone knocked on the door, and a tall, silver-haired gentleman entered, wearing evening clothes and carrying a black medical bag.

"Ah, Doctor Pingree," said Mortimer, still keeping his voice low. "Thank you for letting me summon you so abruptly out of the audience. I appreciate your help. How is Carlo doing?"

The doctor smiled. "Signor Grimaldi is going to be fine. He has a nasty contusion, and he may have a headache for a while, but to be perfectly honest, I think his ego is more bruised than his head. I gave him some aspirin, an ice pack, and told him to rest for a couple of days."

After the scuffle between Carlo and P.J., the curtain had come down briefly, but of course, the opera had to go on. Mortimer made an announcement that Carlo Grimaldi had been taken ill; the audience had moaned slightly in disappointment, but they had no idea what had actually happened backstage. Carlo was carried to his dressing room, cursing vehemently in Italian, and shouting that the opera could not possibly go on without him. But it did. A young understudy from the cast took Carlo's place as Don José, and when the door to the office was opened, they could all hear his clear tenor voice as it rang out above the sound of the orchestra and the chorus.

Mortimer closed the door and stepped aside to make room for Dr. Pingree next to the desk. "I'm afraid we have another patient for you here, doctor. Would you mind taking a look? He had a bad fall when Carlo was knocked unconscious." He motioned with his pudgy hand toward the small figure wearing an immaculate black tuxedo.

Perhaps because he had heard of Angus, or perhaps because he was a professional and a gentleman, the doctor made no comment on the size of his newest patient. He matter-of-factly placed his bag on the desk and opened it.

"Let's have a look, shall we?" he said. He took out his stethoscope and a few other fancy-looking medical gadgets, and began his examination.

He listened to Angus's heart and lungs with the stethoscope. "Take a few deep breaths for me, please," he said. Angus took a few slow, deep breaths.

"Hmmm . . . sounds good. Now, look up into the light, please." He shined a bright light into Angus's eyes. Next, he poked another cold instrument into each ear and examined each one carefully. Then he had Angus take off his jacket and gently touched him here and there, asking him all the while if it hurt. The truth was that every part of his body was sore, but nothing hurt so badly that

it made him squeak, so Angus kept shaking his head no, no, no.

At length, the doctor stood up straight and put his instruments back in his bag.

"This little fellow is badly malnourished and exhausted, but other than that, I can't find anything seriously wrong with him. No broken bones, no permanent damage. I recommend he gets plenty of rest and as much to eat as he wants. Plenty of protein. Cheese, nuts, whatever he likes. Just pamper him for a few days and I think he'll be fine. I'll leave you my card, so if you have any questions or concerns, just give me a call."

"Excellent, excellent!" said Mortimer, relieved. "Thank you so much, Doctor. You can send your bill to me here at the opera house."

The doctor gave Mortimer a pat on the shoulder. "Nonsense!" he said, smiling. "It was my pleasure. I've been coming to the opera with my wife for years, and this has been by far the most entertaining and interesting night I've ever had here. I'll have quite a story to tell my grandchildren in the morning."

The two men laughed as the doctor picked up his bag, and Mortimer walked him to the door.

Dr. Pingree gave Angus a nod as he left, and said, "A pleasure to make your acquaintance, Angus. Take care of yourself."

Angus waved to him a bit absentmindedly. His eyes were fixed on Rosemary. They looked at each other for a long moment, and when the doctor left and the door closed, the room grew silent. Rosemary's cheeks were flushed and her eyes were red from crying, but to Angus she looked wonderful. Slowly, she smiled and lowered her hand to the desk. Angus crept into her palm and she brought him up to her cheek. She held him there, like she used to, feeling his warm, soft fur against her skin.

"I was so worried," she whispered. "I missed you so much."

If Angus were a cat he would have purred, but since he was a mouse he just cuddled up to her cheek, happier than he had been in a very long time.

Mortimer broke the silence. He reached for the telephone on his desk. "I'm going to call a taxi. You need to take Angus back to the hotel. You're both exhausted."

"Mr. Brimley, sir," P.J. interrupted, "I'd be happy

to drive them back. I've got my car, and I could make sure they are safely tucked in. I feel responsible for what happened. It's the least I can do."

"I'll go with them," offered Harriet.

"No," said Rosemary. Her voice was quiet but firm.

"No?" said her father. "What do you mean, 'no'?"

Rosemary held Angus close to her face and looked into his eyes as the others watched and wondered. Angus was stiff and sore, but he managed to put his jacket back on, button it carefully, and smooth his whiskers, all with a rather serious air of determination.

Rosemary understood. She looked at her father, her face glowing and her blue eyes sparkling. "I'm sorry, Daddy. We can't go home just yet. We have a job to finish, Angus and I."

"What?" said P.J. and Harriet in surprise.

"Oh, no, no, no!" said Mortimer. "You'll do as I say and go home. You heard the doctor. Angus needs rest and so do you."

"Yes, I heard the doctor, and we'll go home just as soon as we can. But, Daddy, look at him. He's ready. He wants to do this."

Mortimer began to pace back and forth in the tiny office. He stroked his mustache as he thought about this new possibility.

Rosemary continued, "We can't even imagine what he's been through these last few days. But he found his way back to us. He found his way back to the stage *during* the performance. If Signor Grimaldi hadn't grabbed him, I'm sure he would have managed to get to Minnie and . . ."

"Yes! You're right. You're right, my dear," interrupted Mortimer, his eyes growing wide.

The bleak mood in the office quickly vanished, and an electric current of excitement swept over everyone gathered around the old oak desk.

"They must be starting Act Four by now," said Rosemary.

"It's perfect," said Mortimer, as Harriet opened the door and listened to the music wafting up from below.

"I think I hear the children's chorus," she said breathlessly.

Mortimer bent down and looked at Angus. He was fussing and fidgeting in Rosemary's hand, waiting anxiously for the outcome of all this talking. He just wanted to *go* before it was too late!

Mortimer studied him with genuine concern. "Angus, are you sur-r-re you feel up to this?"

Angus nodded, his whiskers quivering with anticipation.

Mortimer pulled on his mustache one more time. "I don't feel comfortable disobeying Dr. Pingree's orders. But . . . all right! Let's go!"

Rosemary and Angus rubbed noses with excitement.

"Best of luck, old chap!" said P.J., with a smile that lit up his boyish face.

Harriet was going to say something, but she choked up and had to reach for her handkerchief again. All she could manage was, ". . . so brave . . . so brave."

Mortimer quickly gathered up the little group and steered them toward the door. "We've no time to lose. Let's hurry, people!"

They rushed out the door and down the stairs toward the stage.

# One More Time

Mortimer, Harriet, P.J., and Rosemary huddled in the shadows of the wings. As Bizet's magnificent music engulfed them, Angus felt the wonderful, familiar thumping in his chest.

Was there anything in the world more exciting than the opera? The glorious music, the sweeping costumes, the bright colors, the heat of the stage lights—it was all so thrilling. And he was part of it. For the first time in his life, he mattered. He belonged.

Rosemary tickled his ears. Angus looked up at her and saw tears streaming down her cheeks again, but she was smiling at him. "I can't believe you came back to me. It's like a dream!" she whispered. "We'll give them a night they will never forget, won't we?" Then she kissed his forehead and slipped him into her apron pocket.

They were just in time. A few minutes more and Don José and Carmen would be alone on the stage. Don José would "stab" Carmen with his rubber stage knife, Carmen would collapse and die, and the opera would be over. But they were not too late. The chorus was still onstage, singing excitedly as they waited for the bullfight to begin.

Mortimer rested his hand on his daughter's shoulder, holding her close to his side. "I don't need to tell you what to do, do I?" he said, smiling down at her.

"No, Daddy. Don't worry. We'll be just fine."

With that, Rosemary stepped from behind the curtain and into the bright lights.

❧

As it had for so many nights, the pyramid of champagne glasses waited at the edge of the stage. The stagehands had removed the ruby-colored silk that shrouded the delicate pyramid during the day. Now the glasses twinkled in the bright lights and reminded everyone of the exciting possibilities that this night might offer. But more than once Minnie had failed to hit her impossibly high note, and audiences had gone home disappointed.

Minnie knew this might be her last performance in London. Perhaps she wanted to be remembered as the great soprano she was, rather than the singer who couldn't shatter glass without the help of a mouse. Whatever her reasons, she was giving tonight's performance everything she had. Her acting was full of emotion; her voice was magnificent. Her low notes were rich and powerful, and her silvery high notes floated above the entire orchestra.

Angus peeked out of Rosemary's pocket and stole a glance at the famous soprano as she sang her duet with Escamillo. They were so close he could almost touch her. He thought about how she had helped him once, even though she was too terrified to look at him. He owed her this moment of glory.

*One more time, Minnie,* he thought. *One more time.*

Carefully, Rosemary edged even closer, swaying gracefully with the rhythm of the music. Angus looked up and she nodded to him. He got ready. A moment later she gently brushed against the back of Minnie's dress, and Angus leaped onto the ruffles of black lace and satin. Minnie was so absorbed in her performance she didn't even notice when Angus scrambled up her dress, around to the front, and stood on her chest directly under her nose. He felt her bosom rise and fall with every breath she took, and watched her throat tremble with every note. Minnie still didn't see him. She was singing with her eyes tightly closed, enthralled by the beauty of the music.

Angus hesitated. What should he do? After all, this was what made opera so grand: the power and the majesty of the music. How could he interrupt a great artist like Minnie McGraw in the middle of a magnificent solo? How thoughtless. How rude!

Angus could not hesitate for very long. The people in the first few rows of the audience had spotted him, and they were starting to murmur. Minnie opened her big brown eyes to see what was happening. A mouse wearing a tuxedo was standing on her chest, not three inches from her face. Angus did what he had to do—he squeaked and dashed out of sight under her dark curls. Nothing more was needed.

Minnie's black eyelashes fluttered as her eyes rolled back, her mouth opened wide, and her voice went *up, up, up, up!* It rose all the way up to the impossibly high note, and she held it there until the champagne glasses exploded in a shower of twinkling fragments. Still Minnie held the note, on and on. Then her voice slowly got lower and lower, as if she were a balloon deflating, until at last, she ran out of breath. Angus scampered down the back of Minnie's dress, and in a flash, Rosemary snatched him away from danger and tucked him safely back in her apron pocket. The orchestra had stopped playing. No one onstage moved. The only sound was the tinkling of the last few bits of glass as they hit the stage. The audience seemed to hold its breath, waiting to see what would happen next.

Minnie McGraw was not going to disappoint her audience tonight. She was an opera star—a prima donna—and she was determined to act like one. Much to everyone's surprise, perhaps even her own, she did not falter, even for a moment. She didn't collapse or swoon. She didn't throw a

tantrum or storm off stage. She stood proudly, her chin up, her arms extended, as if she were embracing the entire audience. She made a deep, graceful, elegant bow, her dress billowing out around her.

The burst of applause was deafening. The fine ladies and gentlemen in the audience went completely wild: cheering, whistling, shouting, and throwing flowers. Red roses, Minnie's favorite, landed at her feet.

Rosemary discreetly edged off to the side of the stage. She lifted Angus from her pocket, and together they watched Minnie's glorious moment of triumph. Mortimer came puffing up to them, so excited he could barely speak. He gave Rosemary a hasty hug.

"Magnificent, you two!" he panted. "Spectacular!" Then he rushed off to shake hands, slap backs, and congratulate nearly everyone.

Angus looked across the stage. Out of sight of the audience, the entire cast was assembling in the wings. Everyone was clapping and cheering. He found Harriet and P.J. in the crowd, and tried to wave to them. P.J. was busy snapping pictures, but Harriet saw him and waved back happily. His heart nearly stopped for a moment when he caught a glimpse of the great hulking man from the cellar! He had changed into a clean shirt, and scrubbed his face. Tears were streaming down his rough cheeks, and his deep voice boomed out, "Bravo! Bravo!"

The stagehands brought down the curtain for

a curtain call, but Mortimer came hurrying out of the wings. "No, no, no!" he cried. "Bring it up again. Bring it up!"

The stagehands raised the curtain again, and the audience roared its approval.

Mortimer rushed about, pushing cast members out on the stage. "I want you all out there! Come on, everybody! Get out there and take your bows with Miss McGraw!"

The exuberant cast was not hard to convince. Giulio Gatto bowed and grinned. Carlo's young understudy bounded out to center stage next to Minnie, basking in the thunderous applause. Soon the whole cast was onstage. Shouts, cheers, and whistles greeted all of them, and flowers fell like rain.

Rosemary and Angus preferred to remain off to the side, out of the bright lights. They watched the spectacle from the shadows. Beyond the glare of the stage lights, the audience was dimly visible in the darkened theater. Angus could make out a sea of motion—row upon row of clapping hands, reaching far up into the highest balconies. The overwhelming sound of approval made his heart race and his throat tighten in a little knot.

Suddenly, Mortimer strode out to center stage, smoothing his jacket over his round stomach. He and the Maestro seemed to be signaling to each other, pointing and nodding.

"Ladies and gentlemen . . . ladies and gentlemen, thank you so very much. . . ." Mortimer waited for the audience to quiet down. "Ladies and gentlemen, I have one more announcement to make this evening. We have a slight change in tonight's program, which we think you will enjoy." He gestured toward the podium with his hand. "Mr. Hyde-Smith, the Maestro, has something he'd like to say. Maestro, if you please . . ."

"Thank you, Mr. Brimley." The Maestro, looking tall and elegant, turned and faced the audience. "Thank you, ladies and gentlemen. Tonight has been an extraordinary night. We have been thrilled by the amazing talents of Miss McGraw and the entire company of singers and musicians. But the evening might not have been so remarkable were it not for the presence of a very special friend of mine. He has returned to us tonight after a rather distressing and mysterious absence. I'd like to ask the entire cast to remain onstage . . ."

The Maestro motioned for Rosemary to come down to the podium. She looked surprised and stepped further back into the shadows. Not sure what to do, she looked to her father. Mortimer encouraged her with a nod and a smile. Reluctantly, she began to make her way through the crowd and down to the orchestra pit. A small ripple of applause grew louder.

Angus was confused. What was happening now? He could feel Rosemary's hand trembling as she carried him down the narrow stairs to the podium. What was the Maestro up to?

When they reached the podium, the Maestro smiled at them and offered an outstretched hand. Rosemary understood and gently placed Angus in his palm.

The Maestro looked at Angus and whispered, "Trust me."

He waited until he had everyone's attention, then he announced in a clear, loud voice, "Tonight, I'm going to do something I have never done before. I'm handing over the baton to a guest conductor for an encore. Ladies and gentlemen, please welcome my dear friend Angus MacMouse."

Carefully, he lifted Angus up for everyone to see. The astonished audience applauded politely.

Angus looked at Rosemary in disbelief. Her face was flushed with excitement. "Go ahead, Angus. You can do it!" she said.

The Maestro leaned over and whispered to her, "You can join the cast and sing along, if you like."

Rosemary nodded. She looked earnestly into Angus's glistening eyes. "You're going to be brilliant! Just brilliant!" She quickly tickled his ears, then skipped back up to the stage and found a place next to her father.

The Maestro reached into his pocket and pulled out a tiny ivory baton, the size of a toothpick. He handed it to Angus. "I've been saving this for you. This is your night, Angus. The night you've been waiting for."

Angus looked at Charles Hyde-Smith in amazement. Was this another dream, or could this really be happening? His very own little white stick to make the music. Incredible!

The Maestro spoke calmly into his ear. "We're going to turn around and face the orchestra now. Forget about all those people behind you—only the music matters. The music is *everything*! We'll play the 'Gypsy Song,' just as you've rehearsed it so many times."

The Maestro set him down on the podium. "Take a few deep breaths," he instructed, "and whenever you're ready, just tap on the podium with your baton. Remember what I taught you—the musicians will do whatever you tell them to do."

Angus's head was spinning with nervous excitement. His whiskers quivered and his tail trembled. He took three deep breaths, then three more. He was terrified, but he was as ready as he would ever be.

He rubbed the satin lapels of his tuxedo. *For luck,* he told himself. Then he tapped the podium with his new baton. Everyone in the orchestra looked up at him.

With the eyes of all the musicians on him, he suddenly felt sick. For an awful moment he wanted to run away. But then he looked beyond the orchestra to the crowd of performers— and friends—standing on the stage, waiting for him. They were looking at him too, and they were all smiling. Rosemary and Mortimer were smiling. Harriet and P.J. were smiling. Giulio Gatto and Carlo's understudy were smiling. At center stage stood Minnie McGraw, her dark eyes sparkling—even she was smiling at him.

Someone coughed in the audience, and then there was a long moment of silence. Angus summoned his courage and tapped the podium again. He was ready to make the music.

He raised his little white stick and the musicans got ready. The instant he moved his baton, something magical happened. The most beautiful sound he ever heard came from the orchestra before him. He closed his eyes and waved his little white stick in the air. He knew this music by heart; he knew every note played by every instrument.

Soft lilting notes from the harp were joined by a sweet, airy melody from the flutes. It reminded Angus of songbirds and springtime. He let the music sweep over him and through him and around him like the rush of an exhilarating breeze. When he opened his eyes, he was no longer merely Angus the mouse—he was Angus the conductor.

Full of confidence now, he directed his baton to the string section, and the violins answered the flutes with round, jolly pizzicato notes. Back and forth, he made the flutes and strings sing to each other their lovely melodies. Then Minnie's voice joined them, rich and lively, as the Spanish rhythms began to take over. Angus jabbed his baton in the air and the tambourines rang out. He waved his baton again and the wind instruments obeyed his command. He drove the orchestra on, gradually building the tempo and intensity.

In the next verse of the "Gypsy Song," he urged the orchestra to play even faster. With tambourines jingling, Minnie sang about the gypsy dancers falling under the spell of the dazzling music. More and more singers joined in, and soon everyone onstage was singing along, their thrilling voices rising with the orchestra as the Spanish melody began to thunder from one crescendo to another.

Faster and faster, wilder and wilder, Angus let the fiery music possess him. As the rhythm pounded and the tempo built, the voices of everyone onstage soared louder and louder. Just as the music seemed to build to its final crescendo, Angus drove it faster still. Fingers flew over the instruments' keys, and violinists' bows went up and down, up and down, in a furious dance of their own. His baton zigzagged through the air like flashes of lightning, and the frenzied musicians followed, faster and louder and wilder in a dazzling, feverish whirlwind of spectacular sound.

Finally, with a crash of cymbals, tinkling triangles, and singing strings, Angus let his little white stick come to rest, and the last notes died away. He had made the music, at last.

The cast onstage shouted triumphantly. The musicians put down their instruments to give him a standing ovation. The audience cheered wildly. But Angus didn't hear any of it. Magnificent music was still echoing in his ears.

It was the most splendid four and a half minutes of his entire life.

# Epilogue

## Brooklyn, New York, two weeks later

Early morning sun streamed through the small window in Rosemary's room and bathed everything in a warm golden light. Angus had been up since the first glow of dawn. He had already gone downstairs to his little dollhouse kitchen and had his breakfast. He had tried to be quiet when he cracked his sunflower seeds so he wouldn't disturb Rosemary. Then, as he did every morning, he washed himself meticulously.

Now he was back upstairs, sitting on his canopy bed, waiting for her to wake up.

*Lucky, lucky mouse,* he told himself. He didn't

like to think about his dreary life before he met Rosemary. And he didn't like to think about his harrowing escapes from Carlo and Brutus—or how he might never have seen his friends again. Sometimes those memories crept up on him and made him shiver. *Lucky, lucky mouse.*

The opera company had just arrived back home for a few weeks of rest while Mortimer made plans for a spectacular new world tour. That glorious night in London had changed everything. Minnie McGraw was being hailed as the world's greatest soprano. But now, instead of frightening Minnie, Angus would conduct an encore at the end of every performance. Mortimer was struck by the genius of his own idea: a world-famous soprano and a mouse who could conduct the orchestra. What a brilliant recipe for success!

There was even more good news. Rosemary was finally going to have singing lessons, and Harriet was making Angus a beautiful new tweed suit.

Rosemary stirred. She opened her eyes and breathed deeply as she took in the quiet beauty of the morning. Then she smiled at Angus, slipped out of bed, and came over to tickle his ears.

"What a glorious morning. It's good to be home again, isn't it?"

Angus nodded happily.

She looked into his dark eyes and sighed. "You know, I never gave up hope that you were trying to come back to me. You poor little thing. Minnie told Daddy everything that happened. I'm so glad he fired that horrible tenor. Well, let's not think about him," she said brightly. "Look at this!" She held up a copy of the *London Daily Herald*. The headline read, "Tiny Conductor Captivates Opera Lovers." A long article by P.J. Hendricks followed.

"P.J. took a nice picture of you too," said Rosemary. She held up the newspaper for Angus to see. "I'll paste it in your scrapbook for you."

He looked at the mouse in the picture. There he was, waving his little white stick and looking very important in his black tuxedo.

Angus would have blushed, if mice could blush. He was famous. And his career was just beginning.

# Glossary

**Aria:** in an opera, a song or melody for one voice; a solo

**Baritone:** a singer with a deep male voice; lower than a tenor but higher than a bass

**Crescendo:** when the music gradually gets louder and more forceful

**Impresario:** the director or manager of an opera company or a ballet

**Opera:** a play set to music, in which all the parts are sung rather than spoken, usually with an orchestra

**Overture:** the musical introduction at the beginning of an opera

**Picador:** any bullfighter who rides a horse

**Pizzicato:** a technique in which notes are plucked on a stringed instrument (like a violin), rather than played with a bow

**Prelude:** a short musical piece between the acts of an opera; an intermezzo

**Soprano:** a singer with the highest female voice range

**Tenor:** a singer with a high male voice; higher than a baritone

**Toreador:** an old-fashioned term for a bullfighter, torero, or matador

**Torero:** a bullfighter or matador

Catch the next

*Here's a sneak peek at*

# The Pup Who Cried Wolf

## Into the Heart of Wolf Country

Anyone with a good nose and a wild heart can feel the change. I know it the moment we cross the line. Wilderness. I can feel it in my teeth.

Also it helps that there is a big wooden sign that says YELLOWSTONE NATIONAL PARK, and a Yellowstone National Park ranger station with a sign that says YELLOWSTONE NATIONAL PARK RANGER STATION. And the other thing that helps me figure out where we are is the ranger who comes out to the car and says, "Welcome to Yellowstone National Park."

The ranger sounds all friendly, but he turns out to be a rude sort. "Oh, a killer dog," he says when he sees me. He tells Mona to keep the windows up as soon as we leave the ranger station. He probably knows I'll hate that. He says don't feed the bears. Then he mentions some silly law. "Keep your dog on a leash at all times inside the park."

Umm, how am I going to meet my wolf pack on a leash?

"Usually we say that to protect the smaller wildlife such as squirrels." The ranger is still talking. "But in his case, the squirrels might just mistake him for one of their babies that fell out of the tree, carry him back upstairs, and stuff him full of nuts."

Ha, ha, ha. Oh boy. I am so done with this guy. I give him a taste of my rapid-fire barking to show what I think of him.

"Keep the noise down," he says. "Otherwise, I'll have to get out my flyswatter."

Mona starts laughing, and Glory, who has been quiet up till now, starts giggling. And then I hear a snigger. Heckles. That's it. I'm finished with this family and ready to find my pack.

Somehow.

Someway.

Leash or no leash, I am going to escape.